THE
REMARKABLE
JOURNEY OF
CHARLIE
PRICE

THE REMARKABLE JOURNEY OF CHARLIE PRICE

Jennifer Maschari

BALZER + BRAY
An Imprint of HarperCollinsPublishers

Balzer + Bray is an imprint of HarperCollins Publishers.

The Remarkable Journey of Charlie Price
Copyright © 2016 by Jennifer Maschari
All rights reserved. Printed in the United States of America.
No part of this book may be used or reproduced in any manner
whatsoever without written permission except in the case of
brief quotations embodied in critical articles and reviews. For
information address HarperCollins Children's Books,
a division of HarperCollins Publishers,
195 Broadway, New York, NY 10007.
www.harpercollinschildrens.com

Library of Congress Cataloging-in-Publication Data
Maschari, Jennifer.
    The remarkable journey of Charlie Price / Jennifer Maschari. — First
edition.
      pages cm
    Summary: "A boy must rescue his sister after she finds—and wants to
stay—in an almost-world beneath her bed, where their mother is still
alive"— Provided by publisher.
    ISBN 978-0-06-238010-4 (hardback)
    [1. Grief—Fiction. 2. Brothers and sisters—Fiction. 3. Future life—
Fiction.] I. Title.
PZ7.1.M375Re 2016   2015015401
[Fic]—dc23   CIP
                                                              AC

15 16 17 18 19   CG/RRDH   10 9 8 7 6 5 4 3 2 1
                                                          ❖
                                            First Edition

For my former students,
who never stopped asking me
about that book I was writing.

THE
REMARKABLE
JOURNEY OF
CHARLIE
PRICE

I HAVE LOVED THE STARS TOO FONDLY
TO BE FEARFUL OF THE NIGHT.

—Sarah Williams, "The Old Astronomer"

THREE THINGS

*T*here were three things that Charlie Price should have noticed.

For one, the day was blustery and cold. Far too cold for a Cincinnati day in September. Charlie considered it just long enough to pull a jacket from the hallway closet before he walked out the door. The coat was blue. The sleeves were too short, stopping just before his wrists.

It was a coat more appropriate for eleven-year-old arms. Not his newly twelve-year-old arms that had seemed to grow five inches in a matter of weeks.

But Dad hadn't had time to take him to the mall for a new coat yet. So Charlie yanked at the sleeves instead, willing them to be longer.

The second thing was Imogen. Not his actual sister, who was standing next to him, waiting to walk to school, but the one in the photograph on the wall. It was the last photograph they had taken as a whole family. They were on the beach. Charlie had already been a head taller than Mom, who wore a giant straw hat to cover her bald head. Her skin burned easily, even though the sun was smothered by clouds that day.

But if Charlie would have looked closer, instead of passing by the picture without a second glance like he did every day, he would have seen that the image of Imogen had started to fade. Just slightly, as if someone had taken a giant eraser to it.

And the third thing he should have noticed was the dog that seemed to trail behind Charlie like a shadow after he dropped Imogen off. It followed a few paces behind him, keeping an eye on the bright-red backpack that bobbed up and down as Charlie avoided the familiar cracks and juts of the sidewalk.

The dog followed Charlie as he passed the bakery on the corner. As he took the shortcut through the park. As he ducked under the bridge where strange words and symbols were painted in bold strokes and bright colors.

A chunk of Charlie's granola bar fell from the package

stuffed inside his pocket. Charlie didn't notice as the dog gobbled it up but kept its eyes on him the entire time. If Charlie had turned around, he would have seen that it was Edna's dog, Ruby, who sat outside the bakery while she worked. The one he liked to sneak treats to when Edna wasn't looking.

He didn't see her settle into a worn groove between two giant tree roots in the green space outside school, watching as Charlie stepped inside the large brick building that read *Lincoln Middle School* in metal lettering over the doors.

There were three things that Charlie should have noticed that day.

But he didn't.

THE GREAT
T–SHIRT DEBATE

*M*r. Spencer's classroom smelled like math. Eraser shavings and fresh pieces of loose leaf mixed with the slight scent of middle school sweat after gym class. Posters of old mathematicians in stuffy shirts with frilly collars lined the walls, and Mr. Spencer's prized bobblehead collection nodded at Charlie from its perch on the windowsills. Miranda and Rohan were already at the whiteboard, dry-erase markers in hand, racing to solve what looked like some complex word problem Mr. Spencer had projected on a screen.

Charlie slipped into a seat. His seat. Two seats from the front in the third row from the door. They all had seats they had claimed, and Charlie was glad that this seat and the smells and the posters had been waiting for him at the first official Mathletes meeting.

Charlie pulled out a sandwich and a Post-it note that said *apple* from the sack lunch Dad had packed him the night before and sighed. The sandwich was a start—it wasn't made with the good kind of bread Mom used to buy, but it was peanut butter, which was Charlie's favorite. Ever since Mom died last April, Dad had started to leave notes around the house reminding him about parent-teacher conferences and paperwork he had to send to the school office and that kind of thing. But he wrote so many notes that nothing ever got done—which was why Charlie was staring at the word *apple* instead of eating one.

"Done," Miranda yelled as she wrote her final answer, circling it with a flourish. "Three pennies, two nickels, eight dimes, and one quarter." She slammed her marker down on the tray ledge and then pumped her arms in the air. Finally, she put them under her armpits and flapped around like a chicken. It was her signature end zone dance, but for math. It got old after a while, though the first few times were always funny.

Rohan threw his marker down and grunted. "I almost got you that time. You know these word problems aren't my thing. But you give me anything with geometry and I've got you beat before we even start."

"You wish," Miranda said.

Mr. Spencer clapped from the back of the room. "Awesome work, guys!" He glanced at his stopwatch and got up from his desk. "That was fast. Thirty-two seconds. I'm really pleased with how the team is shaping up this year."

"And with Charlie back now . . ." Rohan trailed off, unsure how to continue. Charlie hadn't been able to finish out last year's season. He had missed regionals. That was when Mom was really sick.

Mr. Spencer patted Charlie on the shoulder. "With Charlie back, we'll be unstoppable. Summitview Prep won't know what hit them in two weeks. I think we could be a contender for States this year. Speaking of which, with the first competition coming up, we need to talk about a very pressing matter."

"T-shirts!" June squealed, looking up from her laptop. June took the notes each meeting, and she typically decorated them with a bunch of electronic smiley faces.

Each year at the Mathletes competition, they had a Terrible T-Shirt Award, and Mr. Spencer was especially proud of the fact that they'd had a four-year winning streak. Last year, it had been Charlie who had suggested their shirts say "We Love Pi," with little dancing pi symbols all over them. A few even had actual googly eyes.

"I have an idea," Miranda offered. "What if we have our

shirts say 'Mathletes: Acute Group of Mathematicians' surrounded by smiling angles? All acute, of course."

"Or," Rohan said, "we could put irrational numbers on the shirt—you know, like pi and square root of ninety-nine and the symbol for the golden ratio." He rose up on his toes. "And here would be the really great part." He paused for dramatic effect. "Each one of the numbers would have a speech bubble that said, 'Be rational—no one beats our team!' And here's the even greater part. The shirts will be sports jerseys, and instead of boring numbers on the back, we each iron on an irrational number! Amazing, huh?"

Charlie laughed. It was a pretty terrible idea, which actually made it genius. "I claim the golden ratio."

"You can't claim anything," Miranda said. "We haven't decided yet. You love geometry, Rohan. I thought you'd be all over my idea."

"I like to be irrational more," he replied.

"Clearly," June said. "Should I put that in the notes?"

Mr. Spencer ran his hand through the hair he had left right as the bell rang. It was the end of the lunch period. "All right, guys. We'll continue this conversation next time. But be thinking about which idea you want to choose."

"I'm okay with either as long as they're aqua or neon orange. Or tie-dye!" June said. "We'll definitely win again this year. Five-peat, here we come!"

Mr. Spencer pulled a box off one of his bookcases. "Before you go, I want to give you the official Mathletes folders. The calendar for the year's in there, and so is the parent permission form. Return it to me by next Wednesday at the latest."

Charlie took the folder and tucked it under his stack of books. He had just thrown his brown lunch bag in the trash when Mr. Spencer said, "Charlie, could you hang back a second?"

He nodded as everyone else filed out of the classroom.

Mr. Spencer opened and closed his mouth as if trying to decide how to begin. "I just wanted to say that I'm really glad you came back. You're great at math, and the team needs you. And you know your mom was our biggest cheerleader."

Charlie remembered. Mom would sit in the front row of the competitions, waving her homemade *Go math!* pennant in the air and yelling out random math words when he got the answer right. *Parabola! Equilateral! Pythagorean theorem!*

"She'd be happy that you're back with the team."

"I know," Charlie said. It was hard to think about, though.

Mom knew how much Charlie loved math. And he really did. Sure the competitions were fun and exciting and they always saw who could eat the most pizza afterward (normally Rohan). But what he loved most was how logical math was. Two plus two equaled four. A triangle always had three sides. The quadratic formula was always the same. It made sense.

And even though Mom wasn't here to cheer him on and he couldn't quite depend on Dad to actually put an apple in his lunch, two plus two still equaled four.

Math was something Charlie could count on.

SOMETHING NOT LIKE MATH

1:27.

1:28.

1:29.

"Charlie, do you have something you'd like to add?" Charlie looked up from his watch. Six faces stared back at him.

What Charlie wanted to add was that he didn't want to be there in grief group. He'd rather be in the social studies class he was missing for it (even though they were studying geography). But he didn't get a say when Dr. Miller called up before the school year started to suggest it, and Dad thought it was a good idea.

Dr. Miller leaned toward him. Her eyes were wide behind

her glasses, and her eyebrows rose. She nodded at him, just slightly. Charlie was certain that they taught the look in counselor school and didn't let you graduate until you perfected it. It was a look that said, *I'm here for you*, and Charlie didn't want anything to do with it.

Next to Dr. Miller was Elliott. When Charlie wasn't staring at his watch or concentrating on the exact spot where one linoleum tile met the next, he liked to observe the smattering of freckles that formed tiny constellations across her nose. He learned that she wrinkled her nose when she was nervous and blinked rapidly when she was uncomfortable. Her sneaker tapped the floor underneath their table the entire hour. They were good shoes—the kind you got at a fancy running store, where they studied how your feet moved as you jogged on a treadmill. They were the kind his mom wore before everything happened.

His favorite thing that Elliott did, and she didn't do it often anymore, was when she'd let the smallest smile slip.

It was funny all you could notice when you really paid attention.

"Not really," Charlie finally responded, filling the pause that felt like a canyon between him and the others. He wished he could hide behind his hair, which now covered his eyes and curled around his ears. Mom used to cut it the first Saturday of every month. She had been gone for a lot of Saturdays.

Dr. Miller sighed, jotting something in her notebook, and then clapped her hands.

"We're going to do something a little bit different today." She pulled a plastic tub out from under her chair.

Seven balloons, a stack of note cards, and ten pieces of string were in it. All of this added up to one of Dr. Miller's crazy ideas, which Charlie was pretty sure she pulled from a book. *The Idiot's Guide to Grieving Children*, probably.

She handed each of them a card and a pencil. "I thought we'd each write a note to the person we're missing."

"You mean the person who died, right?" Charlie glanced across the table at the only empty chair. The chair where his best friend, Frank, used to sit. The chair where Frank should have sat now. "I mean, let's call it what it is."

"Yes, good, Charlie." Dr. Miller nodded as if he'd just made some giant breakthrough. "And then we'll send our notes up in these balloons. I rented some helium." She gestured toward the small tank behind her desk.

A note.

To his mom.

Dear Mom, I can't believe you died. Love, Charlie

Dear Mom, I get so sick of everyone asking how I'm doing. How do they think I'm doing? Love, Charlie

Dear Mom, You died and all I got was this stupid
support group with this lady who thinks that she knows
how I feel and she doesn't. Love, Charlie

Charlie crumpled the note card in front of him, crushing it in his fist. He heaved it across the room. It didn't have far to go—the room was small and now felt even smaller. Still, it landed to the right of the trash can. His ears burned even more. "I'm not going to do it."

Dr. Miller nodded again and put a hand on his shoulder. "That's all right, Charlie. We each need to go at our own pace."

He shrugged off her hand and pushed his chair back. It squeaked across the tile. "I'm kind of done with this." He grabbed his jacket and swung his book bag wildly over his shoulder, nearly taking down the cup of pencils underneath the stupid smiling flower poster that always seemed to be watching him with its wide, oversize eyes. Taunting him.

The other kids stared as if this outburst was something new. Truth was, these feelings were always brimming near the top, threatening to boil over. They often did.

Whenever he walked down the hall at school, he heard the whispers. *That's the kid whose mom died.* And when he shopped at the grocery with Dad, the neighborhood women shook their heads and talked in hushed voices about how sad it was.

Like Charlie didn't know.

He yanked open the door to the counseling office, letting it hit against the wall with a thud.

Dr. Miller called his name, but she didn't follow him.

Elliott did.

She touched his arm gingerly, her fingertips like feathers on his skin. "Hey." He turned to face her.

"It was the balloons, right?" She paused. "Nothing says healing like a tank of helium." Her voice went up on the last word, like she had just inhaled some. She smiled a little. "Just be glad she's not talking about the second annual grief picnic."

Charlie couldn't even imagine. Talking about dead family members would go perfectly with hot dogs.

Elliott studied his face. "We could sit out here. If you want."

If anyone could understand him, it would be her. Elliott's brother had been hit by a car the previous September, walking in a crosswalk. A stupid red car that wasn't watching the stupid red light.

One driver not paying attention. One Mom-stealing cancer. Two people gone.

Elliott's face was open, waiting. For a moment, he thought talking to her might help. Charlie shook his head. "I'm sorry," he said, as if those two words might explain everything. He turned and walked toward the restrooms, where he could hide out until the next bell.

"I'll see you at the pep rally, right?" she asked as he retreated.

"Sure," Charlie said, but he wasn't sure that Elliott heard him as the bathroom door closed, leaving his friend behind him.

FRANK

*E*lliott and Charlie hadn't always been friends. Sure, they'd had a class together last year and had been in the same field trip group to the Newport Aquarium, but he hadn't really *known* known her before. She had been more Frank's friend than his.

He pictured them like one of those Venn diagrams his English teacher liked to draw on the board—him on one side, Elliott on the other. And in the part where their circles intersected? Frank Shin. Somehow, when Frank disappeared, so did the lines between them.

Charlie thought a lot about Frank. In group. At home. On the class trip to the science museum. The first time

Charlie met him was in fourth grade.

Frank had stood in the doorway of their classroom on the first day of school, almost eye level with the teacher. She said he'd moved here from Missouri. His pants, a little too short, revealed Superman socks. His shirt had a dancing hot dog on it that said, "Can I Be Frank with You?" If it had been anyone else, they would have slunk into the room, eyes down, to their seat, hoping that if they couldn't remain anonymous, they'd at least blend in.

Not Frank.

Once Mrs. Dunliven had introduced him, he danced to his seat. Not slunk. Not walked. Danced. It was a little bit of break dancing mixed with something you'd see on YouTube and only wish you could be cool enough to move that way. And he sat right next to Charlie and stuck out his hand. Charlie remembered staring at it for a minute. The only people who shook his hand were his dad's friends and his grandpa. Did kids his age really do this? But he found himself sticking his out as well. "Charlie. Cool shirt, man."

From that day on, Charlie would be at Frank's house after school or Frank would be at Charlie's. Frank's dad loved to cook (his mom refused to), and they'd eat kimchi on the porch, listening to Frank's grandmother tell stories about when she was young in Korea. They'd watch Korean dramas played on the Shins' old VCR, and she'd take them to Joe's Bowl-a-Rama every Sunday, even though she never bowled over a hundred.

Frank always said he had two best friends: Charlie and Grandma.

That is, until the summer after fifth grade, when Frank's grandma died.

It was the first time Charlie had ever been to a funeral. In less than a year's time, he'd be going to another one. His mom's.

But he didn't know that yet.

So he stood with Mom and Dad in line at the funeral home, trying to loosen his blue-and-white tie, which somehow felt too tight around his neck. Everything felt too tight. And too hot.

They finally reached the front of the line, where Mr. and Mrs. Shin and Frank stood next to a giant photo collage of Grandma. Dad put an arm around Charlie's shoulder, and Charlie shook their hands as Mom hugged the Shins and said how sorry she was. And then she and Mrs. Shin cried a little bit together.

Frank was quiet.

Frank was still quiet when he returned to school after summer break. Then, little by little, the things that made Frank *Frank* started to disappear. Gone were the funny T-shirts and the goofy socks and the hot wing challenges in the cafeteria. Gone were the times when Frank gave the eulogy for the class goldfish that had accidentally jumped out of the bowl and the math debates they'd have over pies at the Leaning Tower of Pizza.

He could feel Frank pulling away, telling him less, and when Mom would ask, "How's Frank?" Charlie would have to say he didn't know. Mom would worry to Dad, when she didn't think Charlie was listening, about how Frank was doing.

Frank, as Charlie knew him, was gone.

Charlie didn't understand, not yet, of course. He didn't understand why Frank would sit in the back of class, and why, when Charlie passed him in the halls, Frank would just walk on by, staring out into space.

Charlie's mom had given him some pamphlets (probably from Dr. Miller) about how grief took time and how it was different for everyone. Pamphlets Charlie half read and probably could have used now.

It was strange that someone could be there right in front of you, but not really be there at all. And then Frank actually went missing—one day he was there, and the next he was gone.

Sometimes, after Frank had gone missing, Charlie would still get mad at him. Because every time he saw Mrs. Shin's familiar minivan drive down the street, or spotted Mr. Shin at the grocery store, filling up the cart with good food—not frozen dinners or the wrong kind of bread—something red and hot burned in Charlie's chest.

If he had told Dr. Miller about that, she would have said that you can't put value on someone else's loss. But Charlie wanted to because Mom was gone. Not his grandma. *His mom.*

But he couldn't. So instead, he got mad at himself for being such an awful friend and not being able to do anything to bring Frank back.

LET'S GO, PRESIDENTS!

*T*he gym was chaos.

Charlie ran under the tunnel of pom-poms the cheerleaders had created near the doorway for the arriving students. "Washington, Lincoln, Roosevelt, too!" they cheered. "We're going to get presidential on you! Go Lincoln Presidents!!"

Charlie pushed the last of the pom-poms out of his face and looked up at the bleachers. They were almost full. He spotted Elliott near the top. She was standing, and even from where Charlie stood, he could see her eyebrows scrunched in and her mouth pulled into a straight line. June yanked at her sleeve and pointed in Charlie's direction. At once, Elliott grinned and motioned for him to come up.

He took the stairs two at a time and smooshed in next to Elliott, who had smooshed into June.

"This makes me think we need a math cheer," June shouted at him over Elliott. "Like, 'Mathletes, Mathletes, we're the best. We will beat you on an algebra test.'"

Elliott and Charlie laughed. "That'll drive fear into everyone," he joked. "Maybe they'll have a worst cheer competition, too."

"Hey!" June hit Charlie on the knee. "I thought it was pretty good."

The crowd quieted when their principal, Mr. Saldi, took the stage, except for the occasional "Go Lincoln." Elliott's foot tapped against the bottom of the bleacher.

"Good afternoon!" Mr. Saldi said into the microphone. "It's a great day, isn't it?"

"A great day to be a president!" the crowd yelled back. Even with what had happened earlier at grief group, Charlie couldn't help but be carried away by the crowd's energy when the mascot—a tall eighth grader with a pasted-on beard and a stovepipe hat and a suit that looked about two sizes too big for him—ran out onto the stage.

Charlie also couldn't wait for them to call out his name.

"Question," Elliott whispered into Charlie's ear.

It was something that Frank had started. He would say

something like *robots or zombies*, and Charlie would have to choose. That way, if they were ever on a game show together, they'd be ready.

Now, he and Elliott played. Charlie didn't know as much about her as he did about Frank, but he was working on it.

"Who would you rather be? Baldy Saldi or Mrs. Wolfenstein?" Ugh—that was a tough one. Mr. Saldi's head resembled a sweaty bowling ball, and Mrs. Wolfenstein had an unfortunate patch of hair over her top lip.

"No fair," Charlie whispered after a minute. "But I think I've got to go with the Wolf. It's almost impossible to grow back hair, but I could shave my mustache, right?"

Elliott tried to hide her laughter behind her hand, but one of the teachers still turned around and glared at them. "Sorry," Elliott mouthed, and smiled. She could get away with things like that.

Some skit onstage involving Abraham Lincoln and a cougar was just ending, and Mr. Saldi took the mic again. "Fabulous work, all," he said. "It's clear we have a lot of theatrical talent at this school, and if what we just saw was any indication, our football team will roll over those cougars this weekend!"

He waited until the applause died down.

"Now, it's time for us to recognize our fall sports and activities! When you hear your name, stand up and remain

23

standing until we've recognized your whole group. First, we'll hit the bull's-eye with our brand-new archery team." Everyone groaned at his joke.

"Emma Benson, Kyle Bower, Logan O'Neil, and Elliott Roberts." Elliott stood.

"I didn't know you did that," Charlie said.

Elliott kind of brushed it off. "It looked fun, and it gets me out of gym class sometimes."

June laughed. "Elliott does everything."

Elliott crossed her hands over her chest and sat down. "That's not true."

But it kind of was true. She stood up for Pep Squad and Life Scouts and cross-country. Charlie stopped keeping track after she and June both stood for Science Olympiad. Mr. Saldi recognized Elliott as captain. "Were you always in this much stuff?" Charlie asked.

Elliott shrugged. "I guess."

But it seemed to Charlie that maybe she wasn't.

"And now we have the Mathletes," Mr. Saldi continued. "Coach Spencer has told me that this is a team that is sure to go to States."

Warmth spread through Charlie's chest, spiraling out from his heart. Their team—maybe state bound. And he was part of it.

"June Delatour," Mr. Saldi said.

"Yeah, June!" Elliott cheered.

"Miranda Lerner."

"Rohan Mehra." Rohan was down near the bottom of the bleachers, but even Charlie could hear him yell, "Let's go, Mathletes!" while he pumped his fist in the air.

"And last but not least, Charlie Price!" Elliott squeezed him on the knee and held out her fist. He bumped it with his and stood up.

Charlie's grin took up his entire face. This felt good. It felt right.

He felt more like the Charlie he used to be than he had in a long time.

THE SADNESS
OF SPAGHETTI

*C*harlie took his time walking home. The sun had warmed the day just enough that he could push his jacket sleeves up to his elbows, which made the shortness of them not very noticeable at all.

He dug around in the front window's flower box for a key. Two of the flowers Mom had planted still bloomed bright red, even though it was fall. They were her favorite. She liked that she could see them from her place on the couch when she was sick.

Charlie hoped they would hang on a little longer.

Imogen swung open the door before he could even unlock it. For a moment, Charlie thought it was Mom. That happened sometimes. They had the same blond curls, the same rosy cheeks, and the exact same lopsided grin. But then he saw the construction-paper crown on her head and the oversize red heels on her feet. That was all Imogen.

She grabbed his hand and dragged him into the family room. She had set up the miniature stage Dad had made for her two years ago in the center of the room. It had a curtain and everything. "Okay, sit there," she said, pushing him onto the couch. "I need you to watch."

"Are you ready?" She didn't wait for an answer. "Oh, Toto." She hugged her stuffed dog closer to her chest. "I just want to be back with Auntie Em and Uncle Henry. There's no place like home. There's no place like home. There's no place like home." Imogen waited a moment after she had finished, then looked up at him expectantly.

Charlie applauded. Imogen grinned and took an exaggerated bow. "Mrs. Talley wanted me to practice that part. Did it sound like I meant it?"

"Really believable." Charlie didn't know much about acting, but it sounded good to him. "What's with the crown, though?"

"It's for my birthday," Imogen replied. "Lily made it for me, but she didn't want to wait till tomorrow. Do you think Dad would let her come over tonight? We *really* have to practice."

Charlie laughed. Imogen always *really* had to do something. "Ask him after dinner. I thought we could try to cook something tonight. Special. We can celebrate early, too."

Imogen's eyes grew wide. "What?"

"That spaghetti Mom used to make." Charlie's stomach rumbled thinking about the sauce, which was somehow spicy and sweet at the same time.

Imogen got a faraway look in her eyes. "We haven't had that in forever!" She paused. "You don't cook."

Charlie shrugged. "It can't be too hard."

"And then Lily can come over and we'll practice." Imogen's words started to run together as she danced around the room. "Will you practice with us, Charlie?"

"Sure," he said. "I'll even be Toto. Woof."

At this, Imogen laughed, and to Charlie it was the best sound in the world. He just wished he heard it more often.

Dad's specialties, when he got home in time to cook, were frozen meals or peanut butter and olive sandwiches. Mom, on the other hand, always seemed to just know how to make everything. A sprinkle of this, a pinch of that. She was like one of those TV chefs who dumped things in bowls and somehow pulled something amazing out of the oven.

Her spaghetti sauce recipe was just another thing that she had taken with her when she died. Maybe if Charlie's version of her spaghetti worked out, they could have it more often. It could be like keeping a little bit of her alive. Charlie opened the pantry door. A few random boxes of dried beans. An outdated can of enchilada sauce from the Mexican fiesta night they were supposed to have had months ago—another Before. A half-eaten loaf of bread.

Finally, he spied what he was looking for. A can of tomato paste and a box of noodles. He opened it—half-empty. How was he supposed to make spaghetti when they didn't even have enough of the most important ingredient? He felt the tips of his ears start to burn but forced a smile on his face as he turned around. He needed to do this for Imogen.

"This is going to be easy," Charlie said. He ignored the tilt of Imogen's head and the doubtful expression on her face.

"I don't know if that's enough tomato stuff," Imogen said. She hopped down from her stool at the counter, her bare feet making sucking sounds against the linoleum. She hadn't taken the birthday crown off. She opened up the refrigerator and pulled out a bottle of ketchup. "Maybe this would work. I think Mom put in red pepper and garlic, too."

Charlie started a pot of water on the stove and pulled out the spices. He could do this. He scooped out the tomato paste and smooshed it down with a spoon into a saucepan. Then he squeezed the ketchup over the top of it. "How does that look?"

Imogen leaned over the saucepan. "Good," she said. She shook a few flecks of the pepper into the sauce, followed by some salt. "Now the garlic." She studied the container. "This isn't garlic, it's ginger."

Charlie tried to ignore the double-tied shoelace knot that was tightening in his stomach. He was already messing up.

He had pulled the jar from the fridge, and it had smelled fresh enough. "They both start with *G*. And they kind of look the same. I think you can substitute it." Charlie had seen Mom replace one ingredient with another when they were out of something. "Go ahead and add it."

Whenever Mom had made her spaghetti, she had always put on this completely ridiculous Italian accent that really didn't sound Italian at all—more Russian. And she would say, with a white chef hat plopped on the top of her head, "And look at these a-meat balls. One's the size of your head." And they were. Totally huge and delicious.

Charlie looked in the fridge for a thing of ground beef. Nope. No ground sausage, either. Just a few pieces of turkey. Turkey meatballs were healthier anyway, right? He puffed up his cheeks and let the air leak out like a whoopee cushion, just without the noise.

It would have to do. "We'll chop these up and sprinkle them in the sauce."

Imogen wrinkled her nose. "Lunch meat?"

"It could be really good, I think," Charlie said, though he wasn't quite sure he believed it. Beads of sweat formed over his eyebrows. This cooking stuff was much harder than he'd anticipated. Charlie and Imogen watched and waited as the sauce simmered and noodles boiled. The kitchen *kind of* smelled like Mom's spaghetti. A good sign, he hoped. Maybe everything would turn out okay.

Charlie glanced at the clock and then at the spaghetti. "Dad should have been home by now." The truth was, Dad seemed to get home a little bit later each day. Yesterday was 6:55, and the day before that, 6:45. It seemed that there was a direct mathematical relationship between the amount of time that had passed since Mom had died and the amount of time Dad spent away from home.

"Do you want to eat now?" Charlie asked. He stirred the sauce. It was thick, like paste. This didn't seem right at all.

"We can't have a birthday dinner without Dad."

Charlie strained the noodles, put the lid on the sauce, and hoped Dad would come home soon. He wasn't sure dinner would survive the wait.

Forty minutes later, Dad finally burst in from the garage. "Sorry I'm late, guys. I was caught up at the office, and then I had to stop and get something for our birthday girl." He set a grocery bag down on the counter and his briefcase on the floor and winked at Imogen.

"Ooh, what is it?" Imogen asked.

Dad pulled a Post-it from his pocket and waved it in the air. "I remembered that you can bring in a treat to share with your classmates for your birthday." He sounded so proud; that was something Mom had been in charge of. "So I bought something for you to bring in."

Charlie held his breath as Imogen looked in the bag. Her face fell.

"Sandwich cookies." Imogen wouldn't look at the bag anymore.

Dad looked uncertain now. "The kind you like. Right? I thought they were your favorite."

"I guess." Charlie could see Imogen's bottom lip start to tremble. "But not to bring in to share. Other kids bring homemade stuff."

"You could bring them in for just this year and then next year we'll make something."

Imogen shrugged. "Maybe." But she closed up the bag and turned away.

"I made dinner," Charlie said, even though it was obvious. He needed to say something. "You and Imogen sit down and I'll finish getting everything ready."

Dad kneaded his forehead with his hand and closed his eyes for a second. "That's great. Thanks, Charlie."

When Charlie lifted the lids off the pans, everything

looked cold and mushy and gross. Even more than before. But maybe it would taste better than it looked. He dished out everything into bowls and buttered three pieces of bread, one for each of them. "Happy early birthday, Imogen," Charlie said, raising his fork, and watched as she took a bite.

Her lips pulled in as she moved her mouth up and down. She choked back a cough. "This is gross." She pushed the plate away from her with her fingertip.

"Be nice," Dad warned.

"I'm just being honest," she said.

Her words knocked all the air out of Charlie. "Dad?"

Dad took a bite and nodded a few times. Finally, he swallowed hard. "Interesting flavors. A good first try, I think."

"This wouldn't have happened with Mom," Imogen mumbled. She was ripping her bread into tiny pieces, letting them fall like snow on her uneaten spaghetti.

"Imogen, please," Dad said. Though Charlie knew that he must have been thinking the same thing.

Charlie speared some noodles and twirled them around the tines. He shoveled the forkful into his mouth. It was sweet and salty at the same time, but in all the wrong ways. It did taste as bad as it looked. They didn't have her recipe. They didn't have garlic. They didn't have ground beef to make Mom's meatballs.

"This doesn't taste anything like Mom's," Charlie yelled.

He pushed the plate back, rattling the table. Imogen shifted away from him in her chair. He spit the mouthful out in his napkin.

Charlie picked up his plate, and Imogen's and Dad's, and slammed them all in the sink. He looked around the kitchen. Sauce was splattered all over the stove top. The counters were littered with spice tins and leftover turkey chunks and sticky noodles.

"Charlie," Dad tried. "Come on, buddy. It's okay."

But it wasn't. Charlie's chest constricted and his breathing grew shallow. Tiny sparks of light danced in front of his eyes.

Grabbing the jar of ginger, he hurled it against the wall. The glass shattered and sprayed across the room, nicking one of his arms. The tightness dissipated.

Behind him, he heard a gasp. He turned.

Imogen had grabbed her script off the counter and clutched it tightly to her chest. Her birthday crown had fallen to the floor. Tears dripped down her face.

Charlie reached out his hand toward her. "I'm sorry."

And all the feelings that Imogen had balled up inside spilled out. "This is the worst day ever. I wish Mom were here," she said. "I want to be with her. Not with you and not with Dad."

With those words, Charlie felt the ground under his feet

shift just for a second—like how he imagined an earthquake tremor might feel. But he grabbed onto the counter with both hands and righted himself. The ground was sturdy again.

"What was that?" Charlie asked.

Dad stood frozen, his arm reaching out for something. Charlie or Imogen, maybe. "What?"

"That shaking. Did you feel it?"

Dad shook his head. He looked exhausted.

"Must have been nothing, then."

As Imogen's chair clattered to the ground and her footsteps echoed through the hallway, Charlie sank to the floor. He wished he could take it back. He'd rewind time back before he threw the jar, back before the spaghetti, back before Mom had left them and taken everything with her.

A SURPRISE VISITOR

Dad put his hand on Charlie's shoulder. "She'll come around. Things will be better tomorrow, you'll see." Charlie hoped so. "Why don't we clean up the kitchen and give her some space?"

Together, they scrubbed the pots and pans. Dad arranged the dishes in the dishwasher while Charlie wiped down the wall as best he could. He swept the glass into a dustpan and threw it in the trash with the rest of the spaghetti.

Dad surveyed the kitchen, hanging up the last dish towel. "See, good as new."

"Do you want to play a game or something? Or watch a movie?" Charlie asked, but Dad's hand was already on his briefcase. It lingered there for a second, like Dad was trying to decide.

After a moment, he sighed. "I wish I could, but I have to finish a bunch of paperwork for tomorrow's meeting." He paused. "But if I finish, I'd love to." He looked older, somehow. "Thanks for making dinner."

"Sure."

Maybe Charlie could get ahead on homework or something. He unzipped his backpack tucked away under the kitchen counter and pulled out the Mathletes folder Mr. Spencer had given them today. "Hey, Dad," Charlie started. He popped his head into the family room. Dad was already surrounded by papers, a pencil nestled over his ear. "I have some Mathletes stuff for you to sign. Coach says he's happy I'm on the team again."

"I'm really glad, too," Dad said. "Why don't you put it all on the counter? I'll sign everything as soon as I'm done with this."

"Okay, thanks."

Clicking off the kitchen light, Charlie walked to his room at the end of the hallway. It was right next to Imogen's. Her door remained closed, and she was probably still angry. And Dad was going to be busy the rest of the night.

In a house full of people, he felt alone. So he stuffed his

feet into his sneakers, tugged on a sweatshirt, and let himself out the door.

Ruby was waiting for Charlie on the front porch.

She startled him. He didn't see her furry tail until he had almost tripped over it. "Ruby, what are you doing here?" He scratched the spot behind her ear like he always did. It was raining now. She was a little damp, but Charlie found the wet dog smell comforting somehow.

Ruby cocked her head to the side, like she was listening, but kept her eyes on Charlie. Even though they had never had a dog, Charlie knew that most of them had a basic understanding of words like *sit* and *stay* and *treat*. Sometimes, though, like now, he thought that Ruby got what he was really saying. "Why aren't you at Edna's?"

Ruby's tail only thumped against the porch in answer.

"We've got to get you home," Charlie said, and he tried to take Ruby by the collar, but her body grew tense and she leaned forward, like she had spotted something out in the distance. She let out a low growl and bared her teeth.

"What is it?" Charlie leaned over the porch railing and peered out into the darkness. All he could see were the splatters of rain and the occasional headlights of a passing car. "Do you see a cat?" Maybe one had gone under the porch, and that was why Ruby was acting so spooked. Ruby continued to growl, the hair on her back standing up in a little Mohawk.

Charlie shivered, but not from the cold.

"There's nothing out there, Ruby," he said. "Edna will be worried about you." But Ruby only lay down right in front of the door, shifting her weight so that Charlie couldn't pick her up.

"All right." Charlie sighed. He'd call Edna, but the bakery was closed now. He wished he could bring Ruby inside, but he wasn't sure what Dad would think of that, so he did the next best thing. Charlie opened the front door and grabbed some old picnic blankets from the hall closet. Then he arranged them on the front porch like a nest, and Ruby settled down right in the middle of them.

He stroked the top of her head. Ruby could have blended in with the darkened skies except for her white bushy eyebrows, cherry-red collar, and the white-and-gray speckles around her face and ears that seemed to multiply every time Charlie saw her. Imogen always said it looked like Ruby had been dusted with powdered sugar. Charlie thought she looked like she had been sprinkled with stars.

Charlie sat with Ruby, her head resting on his knee, until the streetlights finally pinged off and her breathing became level and easy.

"Good night, Ruby," Charlie said.

And he couldn't quite tell, but it looked like Ruby smiled. The best a dog could, anyhow.

THE DRAGON

The house was dark and quiet, except for the low buzz and glow of the TV. Dad had fallen asleep in front of it again. Charlie took the notepad and pencil Dad still clutched in his hands and set them on the side table. He turned off the television.

Charlie tiptoed into the kitchen and flipped on the light. His stomach rumbled, and all at once the spaghetti disaster came back to him. His stomach twisted—of course he was hungry. Imogen must be hungry, too. But before he could root around in the pantry to see if there were any snacks, a flash of yellow caught his eye. There was something tucked right in the corner of the hallway leading to their rooms that hadn't been there before.

Ignoring his stomach, Charlie walked over and picked it up, turning it over in his hands.

It was a hand puppet. It had a smooth porcelain face with pink-dotted cheeks. Bright-yellow curls sat on top of its head, and it wore a faded red dress. Until this moment, Charlie had forgotten that these even existed. It was a puppet Mom had made in her image. She had made Imogen a whole set for Christmas one year, maybe when she was in kindergarten. There was also a Dad puppet and an Imogen puppet and a Charlie puppet.

He couldn't remember the last time Imogen had played with these.

Maybe she had wanted to play puppets with him. He had promised her that he'd practice lines. The knot of guilt that had settled in his stomach twisted tighter. He hadn't meant to upset her with the spaghetti and everything else. Sometimes he just felt so wound up, like a stretched-tight rubber band, ready to snap.

Imogen's door was still closed, and there wasn't the normal sliver of light that peeked through underneath. Still he knocked.

No answer.

He pushed on the door so that it was slightly ajar. The room was dark except for the quiet glow of the night-light in the corner.

"Imogen?" he called in, his voice rising barely above a

whisper. Maybe he could apologize now.

The room remained silent and he didn't want to wake her, so he just set the puppet gently on the floor of her room and shut the door.

Back in his room, Charlie pulled off his sweatshirt and lay down on his bed. He stared up at the ceiling. Bright glow-in-the-dark constellations spanned out across the dark-navy paint. He had been nine, and after a trip to the planetarium, had been completely obsessed with outer space. Mom and Frank had taken a whole day to help him paint and affix the stars to exactly match the map he had bought.

Frank loved the stars, too, and bought Charlie a book about the constellations for one of his birthdays. Sometimes, Frank would come over at night and they'd use the telescope Mom had gotten him and scan the night skies. Frank always hoped they'd see aliens. "We don't even know what other kinds of things exist," he said. "You never know."

There was one night, after Frank's grandma died, that the moon was particularly full—perfect for seeing the craters imprinted in the surface (or possible aliens). When Charlie asked him to come over, Frank told him in this kind of blank voice that he didn't want to. It was the first sign to Charlie that something wasn't quite right.

Charlie missed Frank. He missed Mom, too. It was amazing

how the sky, which had so many stories, could hold the stories and memories of the people he loved, too.

Mom had loved to tell stories—maybe it was where Imogen got it from. "It's just a small story," she'd always start. But to Charlie they always seemed so big—like they could really happen, even though they were about Greek gods and animals that only existed in fairy tales.

His favorite story was about Draco, the dragon constellation. He remembered the first time she told it. It was a sweltering summer night. He could still feel the heat bearing down on him and the moisture forming on his brow and the cold, sweating sodas they had brought to cool off. He closed his eyes and tried to remember the way she told it, the sound of her voice.

In this story, Zeus, the Greek god of sky and thunder, had taken a girl and hidden her away. The girl's father told his son to find her and bring her home. So the boy traveled to the ends of the earth looking for his sister. He never found her. Knowing he couldn't come home because he had failed his father and sister, he built a new city in which to live. Then, seeking revenge, he fought a giant dragon that protected Zeus's caves. He buried the teeth of the beast in the ground, and they grew to be great warriors.

When Mom first told the story, Charlie had tucked it away. It was one of so many stories Mom had shared. But now, he'd find himself thinking about it when he didn't expect it. Thinking about what he'd do if he was in the brother's place. What it would feel like to lose Imogen.

He wouldn't. If he was the boy in that story, he wouldn't just defeat the dragon. He'd save his sister, too.

REVELATIONS

The next morning Ruby was gone. Charlie had checked the porch right after he got out of bed. The nest of quilts was still there, and warm, but when he ran down the porch steps to look down both sides of the street, there was no sign of her. He didn't know where she had gone.

What Charlie did know, however, was that he needed to eat. After yesterday's dinner disaster, he was pretty sure Imogen was starving. He knew he was.

Luckily, eggs, unlike Mom's spaghetti, were pretty easy to make. Crack them in the pan and cook them until they were solid. Charlie served up two eggs onto a plate along with a buttered piece of toast. He put the last bit of jam on

Imogen's piece. He'd just stick with butter.

"Breakfast!" he called. He had even gotten out the floral place mats Mom loved. Compared to their usual granola bars on paper towels, this meal was downright fancy. He'd have set out a plate for Dad, but he'd already left for work. Charlie had heard the coffee machine running much earlier that morning, before he'd even gotten out of bed.

"Happy birth—" Charlie started when Imogen finally emerged from the hallway, but he stopped when he saw her. She wore floral pants and bright-blue socks and a striped sweatshirt that appeared to be inside out. Her hair was rumpled and thrown up in a half ponytail.

"Morning," she mumbled.

Every day, Imogen had made sure that her hair was just so and her outfit always matched. She and Lily would even talk on the phone sometimes and coordinate bow colors. She probably had the most organized drawers and closet of any fourth grader he knew.

So this—whatever *this* was—didn't make sense.

"Are you going to get ready for school?" Charlie asked, grabbing a glass of juice.

Imogen looked up at him. Dark half-moons had formed under her eyes, coloring her skin like bruises. She hadn't looked that tired yesterday—had she?

He leaned closer. The sharp blue of her irises, which

were the exact same color as Mom's, had dulled like a marble that had lost its polish. He startled. He had seen that look before, but on someone else.

"What?" she replied. "I am ready for school." She held out her arms and looked over her outfit. After a moment, she shrugged and flopped down in her chair. She could barely keep her nodding head from face-planting in her toast.

"Couldn't sleep last night?"

"Oh, what? No, I slept fine." At least he thought that was what she said. He couldn't tell through her giant yawn.

Charlie cocked his head to the side. There was something Imogen wasn't telling him.

"Well, you must be hungry. . . ." Charlie's voice trailed off. There was so much more he wanted to say. *I'm sorry*, for one. *I didn't mean to get angry*, for another. But his mouth just couldn't seem to form the words.

"Yeah," she said. The uneaten toast at her place said otherwise.

"Okay, Gen." Charlie took the seat across from her at the table and waited until she looked at him. "What is going on?"

Imogen looked back down at her plate. "You'll be mad."

"I won't get mad. I promise."

"You won't believe me." Her eyelids fluttered up so that she was half looking at him now.

"Of course I'll believe you."

This time she looked up and stared him in the eye. Her gaze didn't waver.

"I saw Mom last night," she said.

STORIES SERVED COLD

*C*harlie nearly dropped his glass. "You what?"

"I saw Mom." She paused for a moment. Then another. "I knew you wouldn't believe me."

"Like in a dream? Or were you looking at pictures?" Maybe there had been something bad in that spaghetti. Maybe ginger caused hallucinations.

"No, like in person. She was under my bed." She said it as if she were talking about her day at school or a book she liked.

"I know you're mad about yesterday, but making up stories is not okay. You didn't see Mom." The tips of Charlie's ears began to grow hot and tingly.

"I did. She smelled like flowers."

Charlie could practically smell the flowers himself—the earth, the sweetness, the sunshine. No matter where she was, Mom had always carried that scent with her. His nose wriggled. Did he smell it now? On Imogen? No. No. That wasn't possible.

"Stop."

"And then we made cookies, the kind with the chocolate chips and the walnut pieces chopped up really small—"

"Stop!"

"—just the way I like them. I ate, like, fifty of them. That's why I'm so full." Charlie looked closely at her. Was that a piece of chocolate on the corner of her mouth? No, he was letting himself be drawn into this crazy, made-up story.

"And then she poured me a huge glass of milk. I told her I'd split it but I drank the whole thing—"

Charlie slammed his glass down on the counter. "Imogen, stop!" He closed his eyes and clenched his fists, holding them down by his sides. His muscles twitched.

"And we played with my puppets. It was a surprise; she made them for me special. We pretended the puppets were different characters in the play, and Mom helped me rehearse my lines. She can do all the voices."

Charlie thought about the puppet he'd found last night. The one he'd put back in her room. Imogen was acting like she had never seen the puppets before. He thought about not opening her door all the way. If he had just seen her sleeping.

"You. Did. Not. See. Her."

Imogen waited till he opened his eyes. "I did."

"Liar!" he yelled. "Why are you doing this?" And for the second time in less than twenty-four hours, Imogen backed away from him like a startled animal.

She left the toast and eggs uneaten on her plate. In a rush, she grabbed her book bag from the floor, sending papers flying, and ran out the front door of the house.

"Imogen, wait," Charlie called weakly. "You can't walk to school alone."

Charlie didn't know what to say. He didn't know how to deal with any of this. So he did the only thing he could think of: he grabbed his backpack and ran after her.

SCENES FROM
A SCHOOL DAY

Nothing about Charlie's morning with Imogen added up.

Imogen insisted she had seen Mom. Sure, she loved stories and playing pretend, but Imogen wasn't a liar. But there was no way she could have seen Mom.

And so he was back to the beginning.

When they studied geometry last year, they had created Möbius strips—strips of papers with a curve in the middle that seemed like two-sided objects. But when you traced your finger around it, you found it only had one side. It didn't make sense, but it was true. Imogen's story didn't make any sense.

Was it true, though? It couldn't be.

Maybe she had seen Mom in a dream. Dreams could seem pretty real. Or maybe—

"Charlie."

Charlie glanced up, his eyes meeting the waiting ones of Mr. Spencer, who was standing at the board, chalk in hand. He looked around. All the students had turned toward him. He was in math class. He needed to focus.

"See if you can tackle this problem."

He studied the board, numbers whirling around in his head, mentally shifting and sliding them back and forth. After a moment, he replied, "Seven."

Mr. Spencer smiled and nodded. "Indeed it is. Come on up to the board and show the rest of the class how you arrived at the answer."

Charlie pushed himself up from the desk with a sigh and began to shuffle to the front of the room.

If only all problems were so easy to solve.

"Charlie. Charlie. CHARLIE!" Charlie looked up the third time. Miranda motioned at him impatiently. The Mathletes. All sitting behind a table in the cafeteria that was decorated with a giant sign that said *Bake Sale*.

Charlie squeezed his eyes shut. The bake sale. How could he have forgotten? His mind went to the store-bought birthday cookies Imogen had left on the counter this morning. If he hadn't been so confused by everything, maybe he would have remembered. He could have brought those. Dad was right—they were better than nothing.

Charlie lifted his hand in acknowledgment, grabbed some chicken fingers from the hot bar, and headed over. "Where are your cookies?" Miranda asked as soon as Charlie sat down in the last empty chair.

He shrugged, trying to play it off. "I forgot."

Miranda groaned. "Don't worry," June piped up, surveying the table. "I think we've got plenty."

"If Rohan would stop eating everything," Miranda said.

"Brain food," Rohan replied, popping another sweet into his mouth. "Brownies make me smart. Brownies are the key to success."

"Yes, if people pay for them." Miranda pulled something out of her backpack. "This is what we're working for." It was a brochure, bright and shiny with blue and red letters at the top. There were a bunch of smiling people with their hands around one another's shoulders on the front.

Charlie was confused. "The University of Dayton? What does that have to do with this?"

"It's where States are being held this year," June explained.

"We'd get to stay in the residence halls," Miranda said. "Overnight!"

Rohan unfolded the brochure. "And eat in the dining

hall. They have *everything*." He began to read from the list.

"Mr. Spencer told us when we were setting everything up," June said. "He just got it in the mail."

Charlie leaned back in his chair. Normally the state competitions were held in some high school gymnasium with concession-stand food. Now, if they made it, they'd get to stay at a real college. Eating real college food. He hadn't thought that Mathletes could be any greater, but he was wrong.

This was exactly the kind of distraction he needed.

"Cookies for sale," Charlie called out with a grin. "Brownies. Help send us to States!"

Besides Mr. Spencer's room, the library was probably Charlie's favorite place in the school. First, Miss Logan ran the library. She wore these cool combat boots every day, and Charlie and his friends were pretty sure she had a tattoo because Rohan swore he saw it peeking out once over her right sock. But the best thing about her was that she always knew how to find you the right book.

After Mom died, Miss Logan had actually tracked Charlie down in the hallway and pushed a stack of books into his hands and said, "Read these when you're ready."

He hadn't read them yet, but he liked knowing that they were there.

In addition to Miss Logan, there was this awesome loft area in the library that looked like a tree house, complete with a giant tree painted on the wall. It was decorated with papier-mâché apples and birds and other woodland creatures that they had made last year in art class.

The loft was where Charlie found Elliott. Her tongue peeked out of her mouth on the left side, just a bit, which it always did when she was concentrating. She had her head down in the big book of puzzles Charlie had gotten her for her birthday, and tapped her pencil on her thigh. "Okay, if Ron is taller than Louisa but Mary lives in the red house, who is Isabelle's brother?" She didn't even need to look up to know Charlie was there.

"Um, Kyle?" The beanbag chair exhaled as Charlie sank down into it.

"No, not Kyle. He's not even in this puzzle." She muttered to herself a minute, her pencil tapping at various places on the page. "Bob. It's Bob, which means that Ron and Louisa are related, too." She raised her pencil in triumph.

Elliott loved puzzles. Especially the logic ones—the kind where you made x's and o's on a grid, trying to figure out who was taller or who owned the blue house or how old different people were. Elliott liked thinking about the way things fit together. Sometimes she wanted to work on the puzzles with Charlie, but he'd get frustrated when he couldn't get the answer right away or would have to erase his work and start over. Elliott didn't mind getting things wrong.

"What's up?" Elliott asked, marking her place with her pencil and closing the book.

On the way to the library for study hall, Charlie had thought about telling her about Imogen and what had happened that morning, but talking about it would make it seem realer than it was.

So instead, he asked a question that surprised him. "What do you think happened to Frank? Like, really happened?" He didn't know why he asked it. Maybe everything that had occurred this morning was so strange it was making his world feel tilt-y and out of control.

Even though Frank had been gone for months, since March of sixth grade, Charlie felt like he was still everywhere. In the bright-orange Cheetos and grape soda that Frank and Charlie both loved, in Dr. Miller's tiny grief group room, in the red robin Frank had created for the loft tree that was right next to Charlie's lumpy squirrel. Charlie had never known anyone who had gone missing before Frank.

It was a different kind of gone than with Mom. With Mom, he knew she was never coming back. With Frank, well, sometimes he expected him to walk back in the door, ready to solve math problems and stuff their faces with sugar cookies at Edna's bakery. And Frank would laugh at the plaque the school had put up of him in the front hallway by the trophy cases. They had used his school picture. He was wearing a plain collared shirt, his hair was slicked to the side with gel, and he looked so serious. It wasn't Frank-like at all. Not the Frank who Charlie used to know.

Elliott sighed. "I don't know. It's like the one puzzle I haven't been able to figure out. Things don't fit together. It just doesn't make sense that he ran away, you know?"

Charlie knew.

After Frank had gone missing, there had been wild rumors. Rohan thought Frank had been abducted by the aliens he thought lived on the moon. Miranda, who Charlie's mom said watched too much TV, thought he had been taken for ransom money. Channel 5 still ran news stories on him every once in a while—complete with the dramatic music and same headline each time: *FINDING FRANK SHIN*.

"Do you think he could still come back?" Charlie asked quietly.

"I'd like to think so," Elliott replied. "With everything that's gone on, I think the universe owes us."

Frank going missing was another Möbius strip.

And all Charlie could picture was the last time he saw Frank. He could see the half-moons that had formed under Frank's eyes—even through Frank's thick glasses. And he could see the way Frank looked all messy, with his hair sticking out in every direction and part of his sleeve rolled up and the buttons on his shirt askew. But the thing that got Charlie most was the glassy look in Frank's eyes as he stared straight ahead.

It was the exact same look he had seen in Imogen's eyes this morning.

CUPCAKES IN TUXEDOS

After school, Charlie made a detour into Edna's bakery, Crusty's, on the corner. Every Friday, he and Mom and Imogen would walk down after school to pick out something from the tall, curved glass cases.

Mom always picked the sticky bun, smothered in candied nuts and caramel glaze. Charlie stuck with the oversize chocolate-chocolate chip cookies, where the chips were the size of quarters. Imogen, though, loved the cupcakes that were covered in black-and-white frosting. She said they looked like tiny people dressed up in tuxedos, waiting in line for a fancy party.

On other days, he and Frank would stop by on the walk

home. They'd pick a table toward the back of the shop and spread out their homework. Edna would yell at them for taking up space (even though there never seemed to be any other customers), but she'd still bring them samples of new treats she was trying out.

Then one day Frank didn't want to go anymore. He told Charlie that he had to be home right after school. Every day. So he quit Mathletes and he quit Chess Club and he quit homework time with Charlie at Crusty's. Charlie started to come less often then. The empty table only reminded him of what used to be.

Ruby was waiting for him underneath the red-and-white awning over the door at Crusty's. She'd do this thing when she saw him. Her tail would start to wag, and then the wag would travel through her whole body so she'd eventually look like she was dancing.

"Hey, Ruby!" Charlie said. He stooped down to scratch her under her chin. "Did you tell Edna where you were last night?"

"She certainly did," Edna called from inside the shop. Her voice was rough like sandpaper. After a moment or two, she appeared at the doorway. She was moving slower these days and her back was stooped, almost curving into a question mark. She wiped the flour on her hands off on her apron, but her gray hair remained polka-dotted with it. "But Ruby has a sense for these things, you know. She goes where she's needed."

"What do I need?" Charlie looked at her in puzzlement.

Edna huffed and turned back inside. "How am I to know that? I'm not Ruby."

Charlie gave Ruby one last pat and followed Edna into the bakery. He pressed his nose and fingertips against the glass case. Everything looked so good.

Edna swiped at him with her towel. "Hands off. I just cleaned it."

Heat flushed Charlie's cheeks as he took a step back. "But I need to get Imogen a cupcake. I made her mad last night. And I think I made things worse this morning."

"Ah," Edna said. "And you think a cupcake can make it better?"

"I think it's a start. And it's her birthday today."

"You need an I'm Sorry/Happy Birthday cupcake? Seems to me you're going to need a *pretty* big cupcake. I don't know if I've got one of those."

There were rows and rows of all kinds of treats. Charlie surveyed them, finally landing on one. "Maybe the black-and-white one. In the front." He pointed to the largest one, whose top looked like it was going to burst out of the paper wrapper.

Edna placed the cupcake into a white bag scalloped at

the top and sealed it with one of her fancy stickers. "That'll be four-fifty," she said, holding out her hand.

Charlie dug through his pocket and placed the contents on the counter. One rumpled dollar bill, three dimes, a penny, and a button. He'd thought he had more. The tips of his ears started to burn.

"Never mind," he mumbled. He reached out to take his money back when Edna slapped her hand down on it.

"You just leave that right there. Except the button."

They stared at each other for a moment. Charlie shoved the button back in his pocket. He felt the smoothness of it under his fingertips.

"It's your lucky day, Charlie Price. There is a one-time special on cupcakes. This one is a dollar thirty-one." She looked around and lowered her voice, even though they were the only ones in the shop. "But don't you go telling anyone. Else everyone will want a sale."

She winked.

Charlie nodded. Edna handed over the bag. It crinkled in his hand.

Charlie had a plan now. He'd pick Imogen up at play practice. Together, they'd come up with some kind of reasonable explanation for what had happened last night, and then they'd split the cupcake and everything would be better.

UNWELCOME SURPRISES

*I*mogen wasn't at play practice.

Charlie had snuck in one of the back doors of Imogen's elementary school, keeping the bag hidden behind him. He wanted it to be a surprise. But it was Charlie who was surprised when he didn't see her ruby slippers on the stage.

Mrs. Talley was in front of the gymnasium, counting time to a dance number. "No, no, you're off, Munchkins," she said. "It's one-two-three and then one."

Charlie walked up to her, and when Mrs. Talley took a break in between directing the Lollipop Guild and practicing a song number with the flying monkeys, he whispered, "Where's Imogen?"

Mrs. Talley let out a deep breath, blowing so hard that her bangs flew up with the effort. "She told me that your dad needed her to do something at home. She couldn't stay. I'll tell you, Charlie, that's tough. We're doing a run-through of the first two acts, and we need her."

Charlie nodded like he was listening, but really, his mind was cycling through about a hundred different thoughts. Dad didn't need her at home for anything. In fact, Dad had left a note on the fridge saying that he might be late again.

"I'll talk to her." Charlie turned before she could say anything else and jogged to the door. The once-crisp fold of the cupcake bag was crumpled from him clenching and unclenching his fist. Imogen loved play practice. He didn't know why she'd miss it; he didn't know why she'd lie about it.

When he got home, he unlocked the bright-red door that stood out among the other more muted doors along their street and let himself into the house. They had moved to this neighborhood just a few years ago, before they learned that Mom had cancer. When the Realtor had brought them to this one, Mom jumped out of the car and turned back to them, bright-eyed, her hair whipping around in the wind like a mini tornado, her cheeks flushed with pink. "This is it!" she exclaimed. Dad laughed, noting that they hadn't even gone inside yet. "The door just screams happiness," Mom replied. "It's perfect."

And for a while it was. But now all Charlie could see when he looked at the door were the things that had been.

"Imogen!" Charlie called, flicking on lights as he walked to the kitchen. He set the cupcake bag on the counter and hung his book bag on one of the chairs. "Where are you? I went to school to meet you, and Mrs. Talley said you never came to practice."

Imogen didn't answer. Maybe she was still angry.

"I have a surprise for you." Still nothing.

Charlie began to consider dinner. He wanted to have something ready for Imogen. He wanted to prove he could be there for her. After the spaghetti disaster, he'd stick with something simpler, at least for a while. He opened the freezer and took stock of the contents. Frozen vegetable lasagna. Frozen chicken marsala. Frozen tilapia and sauce. Examining each of the boxes, he settled on the two that didn't have a smiling mom in an apron on the front.

"Gen, you can choose between the delicious Salisbury steak and vegetable medley or everybody's favorite, meat loaf with special glaze and rice pilaf. I heard the special glaze is really something." Charlie listened for Imogen's answer, but it still didn't come. "Where are you, Gen? I want to talk."

He thought about the attic, which had a little spot right in a square of sunshine that filtered in through the window, where she liked to sit and think. She was probably up there.

He set down the frozen meals and turned the dial on the oven to 350 degrees.

As he walked up the stairs, his footsteps echoed heavy through the house. "Imogen!" he called. When he got to the second floor, he pulled down the access panel, revealing another set of steps, these a bit more rickety.

Slowly, Charlie began to crawl up them. He peeked his head into the space and called her name again. The pillow that marked her usual spot was empty. Not even the sun was there.

A tiny flutter of panic began to beat its wings in Charlie's chest. He jumped off the steps and pushed the access panel back up, allowing it to snap into place.

"Imogen!" he called, sharper this time. The skin around his neck began to prickle and redden. He loosened the collar of his T-shirt.

Maybe she was in Dad's room. He pushed open the door. Unwashed clothes sat in tiny mountains along one side of the room. Half the bed was unmade, the pillows strewn about. The other side of the room was untouched. Mom's side. Charlie tiptoed over to it, silent, as if he was entering some sacred space. He leaned over the bed, breathing deep, hoping Mom's scent was still there on the fancy pillows she loved so much. He thought he caught a trace of the same mixture of wildflowers and earth he had smelled on Imogen that morning, but maybe he was just imagining it. Lately, it seemed like everything about Mom had been slipping away, like sand through his fingertips.

"Imogen." Her name escaped in one long breath. Still the house was silent.

She had to be in her room.

Imogen's room was dark. He turned on the small lamp next to her bed. Her ruby-red slippers had been tossed next to her dresser.

He inhaled slowly, trying to do the stupid breathing exercises Dr. Miller had taught him. *When you're angry, Charlie, try to think about what emotion you're really feeling. What is the anger covering up?* At the particular moment of that conversation, Charlie really had been mad. At Dr. Miller. For thinking she knew anything about what he had gone through. And now? He felt like he couldn't quite shake the pressure tightening around his chest or the little voice in his head that whispered *maybe, maybe.* Maybe Imogen had been telling the truth.

He walked around her room.

Imogen wasn't in her closet or hiding behind the curtain of her stage. She wasn't sitting in the little window seat with the polka-dotted fabric she loved. The only place left that Charlie hadn't checked was under the bed.

They used to hide under there when they were little

and it was storming outside. They'd listen to the music that the rain and thunder made. It was where Charlie had found Imogen the night Mom had passed away. Those same eyes he had looked into on those stormy nights peered back at him and her voice, a little bit older, said, "I'm scared, Charlie."

Charlie crouched down on all fours and looked underneath the blanket, expecting to see Imogen staring back at him. There was only darkness. But the scent he had smelled that morning—the one that no longer lingered on Mom's favorite pillow—clung to the air around him and seemed to get stronger by the second. He didn't understand.

The flutter of panic in his heart grew. He couldn't stand the pounding of his chest, his burning face, his tingling limbs. What was going on?

He crawled under the bed on his stomach, inching forward like a snake moving through the grass.

As he did, his hand brushed against something smooth and round. He grasped it and pulled it toward him. A piece of the wooden floor lifted slightly, and a small stream of light filtered out of it.

Charlie recoiled and drew his hand back as if he had been bit. The floor fell back into place, extinguishing the tiny sliver of light.

He resisted the urge to back out from under the bed and

run. Clamping his eyes shut, he willed himself to scoot forward even more. He held his breath as his fingers settled into a deep square groove on the floor that he followed all the way around.

It didn't make sense. But it was true.

There was a hatch underneath Imogen's bed.

THINGS THAT DON'T MAKE SENSE

Charlie began to break down the situation like it was a Mathletes challenge problem. First, the knowns. There was a wooden something under the bed. It was the shape of a square. When Charlie pulled on the metal ring attached to it, it lifted. And there had been a dim light.

Second, the unknowns. Charlie didn't know where the light was coming from. Their house sat on a slab of concrete. More importantly, he had no idea why there was a *door* underneath Imogen's bed. He had never noticed one before, and frankly, that was something he would have noticed. And he still didn't know where Imogen was.

Conclusions. Only two.

Imogen wasn't under the bed.

But something else was.

For as long as Charlie could recall, he compartmentalized his memories into neat little filing cabinets. That first memory—sitting at a Cincinnati Reds ball game with a too-large cap on his head and a just-right ice cream cone in his hand and a sticky smile on his face—was filed in the Perfect Days cabinet.

The memory of his mom swallowed up by tubes and stiff hospital linens and squeezing her hand when she couldn't squeeze back was filed in the Things I'll Never Forget cabinet (even though he really wanted to).

But this, this door in the middle of Imogen's room, joined a cabinet that wasn't very full at all. The only other things in it were cancer, Frank going missing, Imogen's outburst this morning, and Dad.

Things That Don't Make Sense.

He slid out from underneath the bed and grabbed the flashlight he knew Imogen still kept under her pillow. Following the beam of light, he ducked back under to examine the door again.

The wood was rough and worn, gnarled like the branches of a long-forgotten tree. Charlie lifted it again. Tentatively at first, and then all at once. The dim light seeped out of it once more, and Charlie tried to maneuver his face into the narrow crack to get a better look. But the space under the bed was tight and claustrophobic.

Imogen was small and bendy. If she was down there, she could easily have slipped through the space like those circus performers who twisted their bodies into impossible positions.

Charlie, on the other hand, was all hard lines and sharp angles. His body could barely fit under the bed, let alone into some tiny crevice. He had to think. He needed to open up the hatch all the way to get a better look.

Crawling out from under the bed once again, he stood, stretching his arms up to the ceiling. Then he braced his hands against Imogen's mattress and shoved, a guttural noise rising from his throat. The bed shifted an inch.

Changing his position, Charlie placed his back against the frame and, planting his feet on the floor, pushed again. He couldn't believe a bed could be so heavy.

After several minutes of pushing and beads of sweat forming on his hairline, the door was exposed just enough that he could open it fully.

For the briefest moment, Charlie considered leaving his dad a note. But he didn't know what to write, and he hoped they'd be back before Dad was even home. So the thought left, as quickly as it came.

Instead, he took a deep breath, opened the door, and lowered himself in.

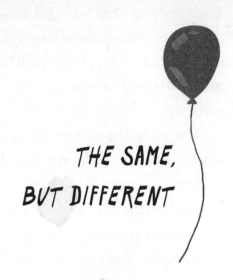

THE SAME,
BUT DIFFERENT

*O*nce, Charlie and Frank rode the Racer at Kings Island sixteen times in a row, only stopping for the blue Smurf ice cream after ride number nine. At the end, when Charlie finally stepped off the coaster for the final time, he felt like a more wobbly version of himself—his legs were made of Jell-O, his stomach dipped and whirled like he was still on the ride.

He felt like that now.

The last thing he remembered was being in Imogen's room, finding a wooden door under her bed, lowering himself into some kind of hole, and now—

Now, he was back in Imogen's room. In the exact same

position he was before—half of his body in the hole in the floor and his arms braced on either side of it, propping himself up.

There was the same red flashlight on the floor. Her musical script on her nightstand. And the quilt that Mom had pieced together with scraps of her baby blanket slung over the side of the rocking chair.

Imogen's room. But how?

He tried to lower himself back in, just to see what would happen. But when he did, he sprang back up, only slightly, like he had taken a very small bounce on a trampoline. The hole wouldn't let him sink down into it again. So instead, he pulled himself up slowly, sitting on the edge of it so that his legs dangled over the sides.

He took a deep breath, trying to slow his heart, which kept knocking against his rib cage, and to still the staticky white noise that thundered between his ears. He tried to sort the information like a math problem again, but he didn't even know what kind of information to sort. What was true? What wasn't? And what exactly had happened when he had dropped down into the hatch?

It was while thinking all of this through that he first smelled it.

The sweetness of tomatoes. A whiff of garlic. The heat of chili peppers. No way!

Mom's spaghetti sauce. His spaghetti had smelled *nothing* like this.

Oh no. Now he was hallucinating. Could you hallucinate smells? This was worse than he thought.

Then he heard a voice. And a laugh. Big and raspy, too big for her body.

Imogen's laugh.

"Imogen," he managed to croak. He said it again, louder this time. "Imogen!"

"Charlie!" At the sound of her voice, Charlie's gaze glassed over, and he struggled to clear the lump that had formed in his throat. He had found her.

His name was followed by the sound of feet muffled by the hallway carpet, and then Imogen appeared at the door, swinging into the room. There was a watermelon-size grin on her face. Her cheeks were flushed pink and her eyes were bright and she practically leaped to him, grabbing his hand. This was *not* the Imogen from this morning.

"I have a surprise for you!" she sang, and pulled him up. "Come see!"

They ran out of the room and down the hallway. Through his watery eyes, he noticed that the surfaces that had once been covered with a layer of dust were now clean. And the clothes that had formed a cascading mountain outside the laundry room were now crisply folded in a white hamper.

And then he heard a laugh that stopped him cold. This one didn't come from Imogen.

He must have imagined it. He leaned forward, an ear toward the kitchen. Banging pots, the whistle of steam, the faint sound of music on the radio.

"Dad?" Charlie called.

Imogen giggled. "Nooope!"

He skidded into the kitchen, with Imogen right on his heels. His eyes went to the stove—the source of all of the good smells and good noises and everything.

There she was. With her curly blond hair that looked so much like Imogen's. And her rosy cheeks, round like polished apples. And the white chef hat plopped on the top of her head.

"I told you! I told you, Charlie," Imogen said. Her arm began to swing, taking his with it. "I knew you'd come find me. Do you believe me now?"

And all at once he couldn't breathe. He couldn't think. Everything he knew about anything flew out the window and took his brain and heart and voice with it.

Finally, a word came. "Mom?"

ONE MORE THING

"**M**om?" Charlie repeated. It was as if he had forgotten all words but one.

Mom wiped her hands on the towel and held out her arms. "Charlie!"

Charlie was certain he would have stood there forever, feet glued to the linoleum, if Imogen hadn't let go of his hand and pushed him forward.

He walked toward Mom. He resisted the urge to pinch himself—to make sure that he wasn't occupying some space between dreaming and waking, when things *seemed* real, but really weren't.

Charlie reached out his arms, too, and sank into the hug

as if Mom were made of feathers. He rested his head on her shoulder and held on tight. Her curly hair tickled the spot right under his nose, and even over the spaghetti sauce, he could smell the light floral perfume she always spritzed on in the morning.

When Mom was alive, she gave the absolute best hugs. She'd squeeze and squeeze (but not too tight—more like she just didn't want to let you go). And then she'd almost let go, but not quite, and really look at you. She always said she was taking a picture with her heart. When she had gotten real sick, Charlie expected that her hugs would get weaker. They didn't. She only seemed to hold on tighter.

This hug was one thousand times better than that. Mom was here.

So many nights, Charlie had thought about what he would say to Mom if he could just see her again. But he hadn't planned on saying this: "So you're alive?"

Mom laughed and Imogen giggled.

"I'll explain everything," Mom said. "But I want you two to eat first. We set a place for you. We've been hoping you'd come." She ushered him to the table, her hand gently guiding his shoulder. She pulled out his usual chair for him and placed a plate of spaghetti on the flowery place mat she had loved so much. Love? Loved? All he could do was stare at the steam rising off the noodles and file this moment away in the Things That Don't Make Sense cabinet.

He found his voice again. "Is this heaven?"

He remembered learning about heaven in Sunday school in St. Cecilia's basement so many years ago, but the teacher hadn't mentioned anything about spaghetti and houses that look like your own and strange transport tunnels in the middle of the bedroom floor. Maybe instead of doing his math homework under the cover of his religion book, he should have paid more attention.

Mom laughed again, swatting him on the arm with her oven mitt. "No, this is dinner."

"Eat up, Charlie," Imogen said, her mouth half full of garlic bread already. "It's really good."

But Charlie couldn't seem to move his fork to his mouth, no matter how good it smelled. Mom folded her hand over his frozen one. He was still clutching the fork with a death grip. It was his lucky fork, the one he always used, the one with a chip in the left tine. He needed something real to hold on to.

"I told Mom about the ginger," Imogen continued, pointing her fork in his direction. "That's where we went wrong. Let me put it in mathspeak. Ginger does not equal garlic."

"Don't talk with your mouth full, Imogen," Mom said. But she smiled, and Imogen smiled a sauce-covered smile, too.

"Is this a dream?" Charlie asked. He felt like a little kid, trying to put a square peg in a round hole. No matter how he sorted the information, he couldn't come up with anything that fit.

"How did you find this place? Do you live here now? How long have you known about this? Why didn't you tell me? Does Dad know?" He couldn't get the questions out fast enough.

"Charlie, I know this might be overwhelming," Mom said.

Might *be overwhelming*? The last time he had seen his mother, she was lying in a coffin in her favorite light-blue dress. And people had patted his shoulder and squeezed his hand and said over and over, *I'm sorry for your loss.*

Loss. Gone. Mom was gone and now she wasn't. His stomach was doing loop-de-loops like he was at the top of the hill on the Beast—something that was awesome and terrifying at the same time. This feeling he had was exactly like that—his stomach in his throat, his voice caught midair, not sure if he should scream or laugh or do both—but magnified times a thousand.

He turned to Imogen and asked again, "How did you find this place?"

He squeezed the fork so hard that he thought it might pop out from his fist. He stuck his other hand under his leg, hoping to still his trembling fingers.

Imogen opened her mouth, and then closed it. He traced her careful gaze to his hands. Her own hands perched on the edge of the table. He knew she was ready to push away from him at any moment. His face flushed red, his anger now directed at himself.

She spoke, her voice quiet. "Last night, after the spaghetti stuff happened and you got mad, I went into my room."

Charlie's face grew hotter.

"I crawled under my bed like we used to during those storms." Her voice lowered even further. "And I found the door. And then I somehow ended up here, where I found Mom waiting in my other room for me!"

He looked at Mom. "I just don't understand what this place is."

"The important thing is that we're together now." She squeezed his hand reassuringly. "Now eat."

Mom was right. Somehow, they were all together now.

Feelings that Charlie had hidden away shot to the surface, threatening to spill over through his eyeballs. "I've missed you, Mom." His voice cracked.

"I've missed you, too, Charlie. So much."

A dull pain began to grow at the base of his skull, right near his neck. It felt like a mild brain freeze, like when he and Frank used to race to finish the giant cherry slushies from Gas & Snacks.

But he was certain that traveling through some strange portal and seeing your once dead, now alive Mom would give anyone a headache. He tentatively took a bite of the spaghetti. Then he shoved an even bigger forkful in his mouth. Now, only slightly warm, it was still amazing.

Amazing. Charlie couldn't believe how a day that had started out so terrible could turn into the best day of his life.

A BELATED ADVENTURE

Charlie didn't think he had ever had better spaghetti. But when he tried to think back to the other times he had eaten spaghetti with Mom, he couldn't think of any.

He leaned over to Imogen when Mom was dishing up more for them. "Gen, is this the first time we've eaten this with Mom?"

Imogen rolled her eyes. "Of course it is!" She said some things after that, but Charlie couldn't tell what because she had just shoved the remaining piece of bread in her mouth.

Of course it is, Charlie thought. But something tickled at the back of his brain like a tag on the collar of a sweatshirt.

Maybe this was the first time they had all had spaghetti together, but that didn't make sense. Did it?

All his questions seemed to disappear, though, whenever he looked at Mom. Her hair had all grown back in. Her cheeks were rosy. She told the same jokes that he loved—the ones that made him groan and laugh at the same time.

Once Charlie and Imogen were stuffed full of spaghetti and they had cleared the dishes, Mom clapped her hands together. "Okay! What should we do now?"

Charlie stifled a yawn. It was probably only six or seven at the latest, though he couldn't find any kind of clock to check. He didn't know why he was so tired. However, he wanted to stay with Mom as long as possible, so he pushed back the tiredness and pinched his legs to keep himself awake.

He still had no idea what was going on, but he knew one thing for certain: he had missed her. If she wanted to do something, he was going to do it.

"An adventure!" Imogen cheered. "Even though it's not Saturday," she added.

"Well, there's always room for a new tradition!" Mom replied. "Let's have a scavenger hunt!" She looked around the kitchen and then brightened, as if struck with an idea. "Okay, you all stay in here and I'll go hide some things and come up with some clues."

She twirled out of the kitchen.

Charlie leaned against the hard back of the chair, resting his head. For once, his body felt loose and relaxed—not tight like a rubber band, ready to fire. Imogen bounced up and down next to him. "This is going to be so fun! I love scavenger hunts."

"Me too, Gen," Charlie said.

"Do you think there'll be a prize?" Imogen asked. "That's the best part."

Charlie was about to agree when he noticed Imogen starting to rub the back of her neck. But before he could ask her about it, Mom stuck her head through the doorway.

"Are you all ready?" she asked. Imogen and Charlie nodded. "I have the first clue." She waved a small piece of paper in the air. "Grab your notebook and pick up a pen. For here you will find stories of a giant and tiny men."

"Oh, I know where that is!" Imogen said, leaping to her feet. "We need to go to the bookcase." She looked at Charlie expectantly. "*Gulliver's Travels*. Remember, Mom used to read us that story about that man who traveled the world." They ran out to the family room and searched the shelves.

Charlie spied a small piece of paper tucked underneath a worn, magenta-colored book and grabbed it.

"You found it!" Imogen cheered. "Read it. Read it!"

He unfolded it to see Mom's large, loopy handwriting. He hadn't told anyone, but right after she died, he took a grocery list from the fridge and tucked it away in his drawer. And sometimes, late at night, he'd take that same list out and trace the words, thinking it somehow brought her closer.

Charlie took a deep breath. "This is the place where we'd watch the setting sun or Mom would relax when she came back from a run."

"The porch!" Imogen said. She turned back toward Mom, who was perched on the arm of Dad's favorite chair. It was weird not to see him in it. "These are a lot easier than other clues you've made before!"

Mom laughed. "It's been awhile. I'm out of practice." Charlie remembered the very last scavenger hunt they'd had. Dad had to write the questions, and Mom could only watch through half-closed eyes on the couch. That time, they had found scrapbooks Mom had made for them with the help of her care nurse. They were full of pictures and tickets to concerts in the park and small memories tucked between the pages. "It'll help you remember me," Mom had said.

"Let's go!" Imogen grabbed Charlie's hand and pulled him to the front door. As she opened it, there was a loud whooshing sound, like air was being sucked away from the house. The sky was dark now. The giant blanket of clouds moving in had snuffed out each star as if they were the tiny flames of candles.

The air was cold, though Imogen didn't seem to notice,

even with her short sleeves. But Charlie folded in his arms a little tighter.

"Where do you think the next clue is?" Imogen said, dropping to her hands and knees and examining the floor of the front porch. But Charlie barely heard her.

Instead, he marveled about how this street looked exactly like his, but it was here and not there. They were on the same front porch, staring at the same cars that lined the streets, the same stop sign on the corner. Though normally at this time, there'd be a bunch of kids playing tag in the yard, and moms and dads standing on the sidewalks, talking. Not here. This street was quieter, emptier—there was no one else there but him and Mom and Imogen.

He thought back to the hatch in the bedroom. Frank had told him about wormholes—shortcuts through time, tunnels through space. Maybe that was what he and Imogen had traveled through. Maybe this was some alternate universe—some things the same, some things different.

Charlie was brought back to reality by a light touch on his shoulder. Mom. "Everything okay, Charlie?" she asked.

He squeezed her around the waist. "Everything's great." And it was.

Imogen pulled out a slip of paper stuck between two slats in the porch swing and held it up in a triumphant fist. "I found it!"

She read the clue out loud. "This is the place you will go to eat. Look on the counter for a very special treat." She paused and squealed. "Is it what I think it is?"

Mom gestured her inside. "Go and see!"

Charlie followed Mom and Imogen, closing the door behind him. As he did, the pain in his skull got worse. But after a moment, the pain dulled and once again, he was left with only a little reminder pinging at the back of his neck.

When he reached the kitchen, Imogen was staring at a small paper bag.

A crinkled white paper bag. Mom reached in and pulled out a black-and-white cupcake, the same kind he had bought for Imogen earlier that day.

"You remembered!" Imogen cried. She threw herself at Mom, allowing herself to be swallowed up in a hug.

"Of course I did!" Mom smoothed Imogen's hair and then loosened herself from her grip. She pulled out a knife from the drawer. "Do you want a piece, Charlie? You two can split it." Mom handed Imogen half, and Imogen took a giant bite.

All Charlie could think about was his own wrinkled bag sitting on the counter. His heart sank. He shook his head.

"The scavenger hunt was so fun!" Imogen said, licking her upper lip where an icing mustache had formed. "I can't believe we hadn't done one before!"

Charlie couldn't either. It did seem like something they would do. Like something Mom would have planned in the past—one of her adventures. His brain strained to remember other scavenger hunts but couldn't seem to locate them. The mental filing cabinet that would have held memories like that was empty. The only hunt Charlie remembered was the one he had just done down here—*Gulliver's Travels* and the porch and the cupcake but nothing more.

The thought sent a little shiver down his back, but he couldn't quite pin down why. It wasn't important, though. The important thing was that he got to experience this one now with Mom, who was here and alive and in his life once again.

ANOTHER GOOD-BYE

*T*onight had been the best night Charlie could remember in a long time. Good food for dinner, folded clothes in the hallway, Mom's smile, and a scavenger hunt with clues and everything.

He still couldn't quite believe it. Every couple of minutes or so, he'd find himself reaching out to Mom, touching her sleeve or her arm or her back, just to make sure that this whole thing was real. That she was real.

"I wish we could stay here longer," Imogen said. She lay on the couch in the family room, stretched out like a cat.

Mom smoothed Imogen's hair. "I know. I wish you could, too. I've missed spending time with you both so much."

Mom moved to stand up, and Charlie felt a little stab of sadness in his gut.

"Are you sure we can't stay longer?" Charlie asked. Saying good-bye the first time was the worst, and now they were going to have to do it again.

"Oh, I would love that, but here's the thing. You can only be in one place, Charlie," Mom said. "You can be here or you can be out there in the real world." She made a large circle in the air with her arm. "If you're gone for too long, people might start looking for you. They might make you stay away from here."

Imogen's eyes grew wide. "Why?"

"Because they won't understand what this place is," Mom said. Charlie knew this was true—he hadn't believed Imogen when she had told him earlier that morning. People might think that they were crazy or making things up. People might stop them from coming down to visit Mom again. "It will be our secret."

"Can we come down again? Soon?" Charlie asked.

"The sooner the better," Mom said. "I can't wait to see you both again."

Charlie went to one side of Mom and Imogen to the other, circling her in a hug. Charlie's mind went to the photograph on the wall at home. The one they had taken at the beach. They were in the exact same positions, only now Dad was missing.

In this world or the other, it seemed like Charlie was always leaving someone behind.

There was no resistance, no spring back like before, when Charlie and Imogen stepped into the hatch this time. They both dropped down into it and, after a moment or two, appeared back in the real house. There was no mistaking it—the sweet, flowery scent of Mom was gone. And though it was still dark out, when Charlie's eyes adjusted, he could see the pile of laundry in the corner and Imogen's unmade bed.

Even though his stomach was full from the spaghetti, he felt empty again. That hole opening back up underneath his skin that only being with Mom could fill. He missed her already.

Charlie braced his arms against the side of the hatch and pulled himself up. He grabbed Imogen's hands to help her but eventually had to lift her from under her armpits because she had grown limp and heavy. It was late. He was sure that Imogen was exhausted. According to the glowing clock on her dresser, it was 3:05 in the morning.

He helped her to her bed and slipped off her gym shoes. He grabbed the blanket off her rocking chair and tucked it around her. Out of the corner of his eye, he caught her ruby slippers sitting next to her backpack. The musical. He turned to ask her about it, but she was already softly snoring, her curls a wild halo around her face. He'd have to talk to her about it tomorrow.

Charlie closed the hatch quietly, letting the wooden door latch back into place. Right before he left the room, he doubled back. He took a giant stack of the heaviest books from Imogen's bookshelf and placed them on top.

If Charlie and Imogen could travel to some alternate world, maybe things could travel to theirs. He didn't know everything about how it worked yet, and he didn't want strange creatures he didn't know or trust climbing up through the hatch. Mom he could trust; other things, he wasn't so sure.

There was probably nothing to worry about.

But he wanted to be certain, just in case.

SATURDAYS

When his family wasn't busy having their adventures Mom had planned, Charlie and Frank would grab their bikes and ride all around their neighborhood. They'd eat bagels at the park, and then they'd swing by Rohan's house to play video games or watch a monster movie.

These Saturdays disappeared before Frank did. One Saturday, Charlie sat by the door all morning, waiting for Frank to ring the doorbell like he always had. And Frank didn't. And when Charlie called him, Frank didn't pick up, and he didn't say anything about it that following Monday at school either. In fact, he didn't say anything to him at school at all.

So when the doorbell rang that Saturday morning, Charlie shot up in bed. Then he groaned. His legs and arms were a little achy and his head was stuffed with cotton. For a moment, that was all his brain could focus on—he felt like he was coming down with something, a cold or maybe the flu. Then at once, it all came back. Last night and Mom and spaghetti. The passageway under Imogen's bed. The little headache that was lingering today. Maybe it had all been a strange dream, though his legs and head said otherwise.

He stumbled out of bed and down the hall into Imogen's room. She was still asleep. He fell down onto his hands and knees next to the hatch and pushed aside the books he had set there the night before. He traced the edge where the wood door of the hatch met the floor. It was real. It was all real. He sat back and ran his hands through his hair. Mom was down there. Mom was back!

The doorbell rang again.

Imogen didn't stir and he didn't hear Dad moving about, so Charlie scrambled to his feet and ran down the hallway, past the picture wall, to the front door. He opened it without even looking out through the peephole.

It was Elliott. And Ruby.

Ruby first tried to nose her way in the door past Charlie. "Ruby, no." Charlie laughed, but Ruby didn't stop, and he had to grab her by her cherry collar and turn her back out the door.

"Hey," Charlie said, looking up at Elliott. Moving around was helping the fog clear from his head.

He glanced past her at the bike she had propped against the front porch. It was blue and yellow with racing stripes down the side. She saw him looking and laughed. "I got a new bike. Do you want to ride around?" She tapped her sneaker up down, up down.

"With you and Ruby?" Charlie asked.

Elliott shrugged. "She was already here when I rode up, waiting on the porch."

Strange. Ruby waiting for him again. He remembered Edna's words—Ruby always went where she was needed. What did Charlie and Imogen need now that Mom was back in their lives?

He looked back to Elliott. What Charlie really wanted to do was go back down and see Mom again. But he couldn't go too often. Or stay too long. That's what Mom had said. And a ride with Elliott did sound great. What would be even better was if Frank pulled up a moment later and they all went together. If anything, last night had taught him that the impossible could happen.

"Yeah, just give me two minutes." Charlie closed the door and ran back down the hall. He grabbed his toothbrush out of the bathroom and popped into Imogen's room.

"Do you want to go on a bike ride with me and Elliott? Ruby's coming, too."

Imogen groaned and put one of her pillows over her head. Normally, she would have beaten him out the door. She loved Elliott and was certain that Ruby was made of magic.

"Come on, Imogen. It will be fun. Maybe we'll even get some Skyline for lunch," Charlie said. That was sure to convince her. Imogen loved getting the chili dogs with extra cheese and onions—the more hot sauce the better.

"I don't really feel like it," came her muffled reply.

"Okay," Charlie said. He lingered at Imogen's door a second—maybe he should stay. But then he heard Ruby's bark and Elliott's laughter and decided it would be okay if he went for just a little while. "We won't be gone too long." He finished brushing his teeth and changed into jeans and a fresher-smelling T-shirt he retrieved from the laundry pile.

"Are you sure?" he called one last time.

Imogen didn't answer.

The air was crisp and cool—the kind of air that makes all your nerve endings tingle. The sun was bright overhead and the light streamed through the trees, making the leaves seem greener and oranger and redder than normal. Everything seemed alive. Charlie felt alive.

As they pedaled down Allston Street, Charlie felt like his bicycle had grown wings. The wind was in his face, threading through his hair, lifting his jacket up at the waist. He and Elliott raced down the streets, zigging this way and that, Ruby close behind. Elliott veered left toward Tiny Meadows. They jumped off the bikes, leaving them at the edge of the playground, wheels still turning.

Charlie spun Elliott on the roundabout. Her ponytail whipped through the air. Her laughter filled the space between them. Faster and faster she flew until Charlie let go and they both stumbled to the ground, gasping for air. Ruby lay down next to Charlie, her body warm. She licked the tears that had formed on Elliott's windburned face.

They all lay there, staring up at the clouds that ambled across the sky, and Charlie marveled at how free he felt. Before it was like he had been under piles and piles of thick blankets. He had never noticed until this moment, when nothing weighed on him at all.

"Do you think that cloud looks like a hot dog?" Elliott asked.

Charlie laughed. "I was thinking more of a banana, but I think it means we're both hungry."

They biked over to the Skyline. Elliott got the chili spaghetti with extra oyster crackers. Charlie got two chili dogs, and they made sure to get a plain hot dog for Ruby. They grabbed a patio table so Ruby could sit with them and leaned their bikes against the brick building.

Elliott broke open the top of an oyster cracker, dotted the top with a bubble of hot sauce, and popped it into her mouth. She followed it with a forkful of spaghetti.

"You know," she said, "I love this, but your mom's spaghetti was even better."

Charlie froze, mid-chew. He inhaled sharply and then coughed, the hot dog almost getting stuck in his throat. Elliott reached over to pound him on the back.

"Are you okay?"

"Fine," Charlie wheezed. He took a big swig of his soda. Mom's spaghetti. But last night was the first night they had eaten it with her, and Elliott didn't know anything about that. "What do you mean, Mom's spaghetti?"

A confused look passed over Elliott's face. "Remember— we made that volcano together for class, and she made us dinner. Her meatballs were the best."

It all sounded familiar, but as much as Charlie searched and searched his brain, he couldn't remember eating it any time before last night. The sensation in his brain at that moment was like reaching for a word that you could almost think of, but not quite, and then days later it finally came to you, but then it was too late. He could feel Elliott's and Ruby's eyes on him.

"Yeah, of course," Charlie said. He didn't feel quite as light anymore. Why couldn't he remember it? Elliott did. But he couldn't admit that to her without explaining everything, so he said, "That was so fun."

He wanted to tell Elliott everything that had happened the night before, this huge secret that seemed to push on him from the inside out. But Mom had wanted to keep it between them, and even if she hadn't, Elliott might not even believe him. They were quieter as they finished their food. Now the day seemed a little colder, the leaves a little more dull, and the sun didn't shine so bright.

"Can you come back and hang out?" Charlie asked.

Elliott shook her head. "Cross-country meeting, and then we have a campout for Life Scouts. I'm in charge of the s'mores."

Charlie rode alongside Elliott back to her house. Then, hopping off his bike, Charlie walked it the rest of the way alone, with only Ruby, his thoughts, and the *clank clank clank* of the front wheel's broken spoke to keep him company. When they got back to his front porch, Charlie sat on the step. Some of the paint was peeling and he picked at it with his fingernail. Ruby sat beside him, leaning all her weight into him.

"So Mr. Spencer has these math problems that he gives us in class every Friday," Charlie began. Ruby tilted her head like she was listening. "And they're pretty impossible. Last year, I only got five right. Five! And that was more than anyone else in the class."

He knew Mom had told him not to tell anyone about her and the hatch and the world below (or wherever it was), but Ruby wasn't a person. Ruby was a dog. And dogs couldn't tell anyone anything, so he thought sharing with her might be okay.

"That's what this is like, Ruby." He lowered his voice. "Last night Imogen and I went down a hatch, and I think we went to some alternate world. Where Mom is alive."

Ruby growled.

"No, no, it's not like that," Charlie said. "It's not like she's a zombie or something. She's normal. She made us spaghetti, and we had a scavenger hunt. It was just like old times. At least I think it was. I think we had spaghetti dinners and scavenger hunts with her before. I just can't remember."

He paused, thinking for a moment. "I just don't know why I can't remember. Imogen and I are going to go down again tonight to visit. Maybe I'll ask Mom then."

Charlie stood up but then fell to the steps again. Ruby had latched onto his pant leg with her teeth.

At first he laughed. He scratched her again right where she liked it. "Come on, girl, time to go." But she still wouldn't let go of his jeans. Finally he said, "Ruby, stop playing. I need to get inside, and you need to get back to Edna." He yanked his pants leg away. "I don't know why you're acting so weird."

This wasn't the Ruby he knew—from the sleeping on the porch to the growling and now this.

"Okay, go home now," Charlie said. But when he closed the front door behind him, Ruby hadn't moved an inch.

SLEEPING BEAUTY

Imogen was still asleep. It had been almost two hours since Charlie had left the house, and it was now one thirty. Rohan always bragged to the rest of the Mathletes about how long he could sleep in on the weekends, but this was way past that. And this was Imogen.

He flipped on the light in Imogen's room. "Imogen, it's time to get up."

She didn't answer.

He walked up to her and shook her shoulder. She stirred, rolled over, and opened her eyes. For the second time that day, he breathed in sharply. When she looked at him, it was like she was looking past him. Like she couldn't see him at all.

"Is it time to go visit Mom again?" she asked groggily.

"No, not yet," he said.

She rolled back over. "Wake me up when it is."

Charlie pulled her toward him. "Uh, no, no, no. You need to get up now." He had been tired when he had woken up earlier, but nothing like this. What was going on?

He pushed Imogen up in bed so she was sitting. She flopped back down. "Imogen," Charlie said. He tried to make his voice sound stern. "I'm going to go start the shower for you, and when I get back, you need to be out of bed."

Maybe Imogen was feeling sick like he had this morning. When they hadn't felt good, Mom always had them take a shower or a bath, and it somehow made them magically feel better. Charlie hoped it would work this time for Imogen.

He turned on the water and tested it to make sure it wasn't too hot. Then he counted to twenty, just to give her more time, and walked back into her room. She had managed to pull a sweatshirt and polka-dot pants from her drawer, but they were now on the floor and she was back in bed.

This time, he yanked her up and forced her to stand. She kind of collapsed into him, her arms barely touching the tops of his shoulders. He grabbed her clothes from the floor and dragged her to the bathroom, her feet making track marks in the hallway carpet.

At the bathroom door, he gently pushed her in and set her clothes on the bathroom rug. "Okay, Imogen," he yelled through the door. "This is as much as I can help. But you can't just lie on the floor in there. You actually have to take a shower." He pressed his ear against the wood and waited to hear the curtain be pulled aside and for her to step in. After a minute or two, she did. He let out a big breath.

He sank to the carpet. His afternoon with Elliott had lost some of its shine. His mind kept returning to the moment at lunch with her and the spaghetti and why he couldn't remember what she remembered.

And Imogen kept acting more and more *not* like Imogen. He kept thinking about that, too.

He wished he could stop being so logical about things. He wished that they could all be together—Mom and Dad, Imogen and Charlie—but like the old versions of themselves, not these disjointed strange ones.

He stood up and pulled down the photograph of them at the beach, so he could remember, and he blinked.

He blinked again.

Something was wrong with the picture.

He walked to the end of the hallway. There was better light there.

He held it up, catching a bit of the sun. His brain wasn't playing tricks. There they were—Dad and Mom and Charlie and Imogen. The beach and the gray sky. The shore in the background. But Imogen—while the rest of the photograph was still sharp and colorful, and the outlines of Dad and Mom clear—Imogen was muted, faded, almost as if she were disappearing into the background.

While Charlie wasn't quite as faded as Imogen, the lines around his body had softened as well, his coloring a little less bright.

His mind went through the obvious explanations.

It had faded in the sun. But the hallway didn't have direct light, and if that was true, wouldn't the entire photograph fade?

Charlie hurried to the other photographs lining the hallway.

He bounced from one to the other in a rapid motion, as if he were stuck in a pinball machine. And in each one, he and Imogen had both faded. He had no idea what this meant.

Charlie didn't assume that finding Mom in the other world and the strangeness in the pictures had anything to do with each other. They could simply be coincidences.

But still, he once again found himself in a place where he didn't like to be.

A place where he didn't have all the answers.

OUT OF BALANCE

A little later that afternoon, Charlie and Imogen sat on the couch. Charlie had been attempting to study for his invertebrates test on Monday, but after he had reread page fifty-four in his textbook three times, he put it aside. The only things he could think about were getting back to Mom and Imogen. Imogen did look a little better. She had some color back in her cheeks and was actually awake, which seemed like a pretty big step at this point.

"Is it time to go see Mom?" Imogen asked. This was the fifth time she had asked over the span of an hour—Charlie had counted.

"You remember what Mom said. We can't be gone all

the time, or people will start to wonder. Dad has to actually *see* us."

Imogen frowned.

Charlie knew he needed to change the subject. "We could practice for the play. I could be the Lion or the Tin Man. Or even the Wicked Witch of the West." He bent his hands into claw shapes. "I'll get you, my pretty," he cackled. Then: "I'm melting. I'm melting!"

Imogen didn't crack a smile. "I don't really feel like it."

Charlie tried again. "You could invite Lily over and maybe Min—she's playing the aunt, right? We could do a whole show here in the living room. Mrs. Talley was worried about you on Friday. You've got to be ready for Monday's practice."

"I don't want to invite anyone over, and I'm not going Monday."

"But you have to go Monday," Charlie said.

Imogen picked at the blanket on the couch, separating out each piece of fringe. "It's just not important anymore."

It's just not important anymore. The words echoed in Charlie's ears. Wasn't that what Frank had said once upon a time about Mathletes and Chess Club? And even though he didn't want to make the connection, he had to. Finding Mom and the strangeness in the pictures and now Imogen's words. This was a third thing. Not all of these things could be coincidences. They had to be related in some way.

During the Mathletes district championship last March, there had been one final problem to win the entire thing. As soon as the judge read it out loud, Charlie's brain began moving information around. Grouping. Regrouping. Crossing things out. Adding numbers together. Rethinking. Reworking.

Until finally, he realized he was missing something very obvious. And then all the pieces fit together and the answer clicked into place and Charlie buzzed in.

Charlie felt like that now. He wasn't quite ready to buzz in. Yet. But he knew there was something *to* know. Pieces to be fit together, answers to click into place.

Before he could think more on it, the garage door opened. A moment later, Dad walked into the room and collapsed on the chair. "What a day!" he said. He closed his eyes for a moment and then opened them, right at Charlie.

"Hey, did you know that there's a dog on our front porch?"

Charlie nodded. Ruby. She must still be out there. He looked at Imogen. He hadn't told her about Ruby. Old Imogen would have run outside that very second to smother her with kisses. Not this Imogen. This Imogen didn't even seem to register what was going on.

"So I thought that maybe we could get some pizza tonight," Dad said. He hadn't noticed Imogen's silence. Or maybe he had and had chosen to pretend it wasn't happening. "We haven't had LaRosa's in a long time. We could call it in or even go eat there."

At this, Imogen's ears did perk up.

"We're not that hungry, Dad," she said.

Charlie turned to her, his jaw slack. Dad wasn't working or sleeping in front of the TV or forgetting something—he was actually asking to do something with them. Something that they used to do. Something as a family.

But Imogen narrowed her eyes and motioned with her head toward her room, just slightly, so that only Charlie picked up on it.

Charlie hesitated, but Imogen's stare only intensified.

"Maybe another time, Dad. We're actually really tired—I think we might go to bed early."

Imogen yawned in emphasis.

"It's only five o'clock." Charlie could see the confusion on Dad's face, and a little bit of him crumpled inside.

Imogen shrugged. "You're not normally home by now." She got up from the couch, stretched, and walked past Dad without a backward glance. Charlie stood to follow her.

"Next weekend for sure, Dad," Charlie said.

Charlie hated leaving Dad like this. But he also couldn't wait to see Mom, even though he had more questions than before.

STORE—BOUGHT POTATOES

Frank's grandma had really loved infomercials on TV. His family was always getting some kind of package in the mail—the Spicy Shelf, a self-cleaning fish tank (even though they didn't have any fish), and a fine pair of pajama jeans, which, according to Grandma, were quite comfortable. It struck Charlie how much the hatch was like the commercial for one of the products. Before Imogen was full of yawns and drooping shoulders and eyes that seemed glassy and dazed. But one trip through the hatch and *presto chango*, New Imogen emerged with smiles and enough bounce that she seemed to be filled with soda bubbles.

Once again, the other house smelled delicious. If Mom's spaghetti was a 10, then her meat loaf was a 9.7. She would always put the crunchy onions on top and serve it with mashed potatoes that she had smooshed up herself. After she died, Charlie tried to make potatoes from a box one night after everyone was asleep. He just wanted to taste them one more time.

They weren't the same.

"Meat loaf!" Imogen exclaimed. She pulled out her chair and immediately sat down, fork in hand. "I'm ready!" she added, in an especially loud voice.

"Hold your horses!" Mom laughed. "Don't I get a hug first?" She rounded the counter and leaned down to embrace Imogen. Then she turned to Charlie, who was still leaning against the kitchen wall. "And now my boy, whose hair has gotten so long!" She reached out to ruffle his hair, but Charlie found himself ducking away. He couldn't seem to stop thinking about the strange connection between Imogen and Frank and the pictures in the hallway and the not being able to remember things.

A look crossed Mom's face that he couldn't quite read. Was she annoyed?

Charlie chided himself. Of course she was. Here he was avoiding Mom, who before last night, he hadn't seen for months. *Because she had died.* He pushed the thought down, down, down through his body and forced himself to extend his arms.

But this hug? It was kind of like the mashed potatoes from the box. It wasn't quite the same.

From the way his teeth were clenched, Charlie knew his grin was strained. Luckily, though, Mom didn't seem to notice. Instead she put two steaming plates of meat loaf and mashed potatoes and the good kind of rolls on the table.

"Aren't you going to eat?" Charlie asked. He glanced up at her.

There was that look again! But as quickly as it appeared, it vanished.

"I had some before you both came," Mom said. "You took so long to get here."

"I know," Imogen said between bites. "Charlie said we had to wait till Dad got home, and then he was trying to make me take a shower and talk about the play, but I was just so tired."

"How do you feel now?" Mom asked.

"Much better," Imogen said. "I love being with you."

"What about you, Charlie?" Mom asked.

Charlie thought for a moment. Last night, when he had first traveled here, seemed like light-years away. "I love seeing you, Mom." His voice trailed off. He really did love seeing her. But maybe what he didn't love was everything else that seemed to come with it.

They finished dinner in silence, with Imogen not taking her eyes off Mom, Charlie concentrating extra hard on his meat loaf, and Mom looking at Charlie with a raised eyebrow he could see in the reflection off his plate.

Charlie offered to do the dishes after dinner while Mom and Imogen set up the Scrabble board in the family room. Just before they entered the hatch, Imogen had asked him to grab it. It had been one of their favorite things to do. He picked up the first plate and set it down in the sink. The pain in his head had started right after dinner again, but this time it hadn't dulled like before. He watched the water run over his hands and down the drain. Where did the water in this place go? This time, he didn't ignore his brain when it said, *Look closer, look closer.* Leaving the water on, he crept past the door to the family room, shooting a quick glance at Mom and Imogen. They were only unpacking the tiles from the bag and wouldn't expect him to be done for a few minutes.

Charlie knew exactly where he wanted to look first. He rounded the corner into the front hallway, where the pictures lined the walls. They were the same ones from the real house. Imogen on her first day of kindergarten. Charlie holding up a Mathletes trophy. Their family at the beach.

In each of the pictures, Imogen and Charlie's shapes

were still faded, though Imogen's lines were a bit sharper here in the real world. While Charlie still looked ghost-like, Imogen looked more like she belonged.

There was something else different, too. Something bigger. Mom. Imogen. Charlie. And instead of Dad, there was a Dad-sized hole where he should be. He rubbed his eyes and looked again. Still no Dad.

He looked at another picture—the one with him and Dad at the Mathletes tournament. But this one just had Charlie.

Dad wasn't in any of these pictures.

Before he could think on it further, he heard a noise in the kitchen. The dishes! How long had he been out here?

He raced back, his socks sliding on the linoleum. He skidded to a stop against the counter when he saw who was waiting for him. Oh man.

"Where were you, Charlie?" Mom asked. There was an edge to her voice.

He would ask her. He would ask her about the pictures in the hallway, and she would explain everything, and it would make total sense. But something in his gut told him not to. He wanted to figure out more on his own. "The bathroom." He shrugged. "I had to go."

Now he recognized a new look on her face. Suspicion.

"I'll just finish up in here and will be out in a second.

Don't start without me."

Mom looked like she wanted to say something else but didn't. Instead, she turned and walked back into the family room. Charlie let out a sigh that was swallowed up by the running water.

He had all these different pieces that seemed to be adding up to a whole lot of nothing. Even with that, though, Charlie knew one thing for sure—his brain had won out.

Dad liked to use this phrase—*there's no such thing as a free lunch*. And he'd say it at the most annoying times, like when Charlie was really excited about getting this free airplane kit in the mail. Dad meant that everything had a price.

Charlie had been so excited to see Mom.

But now, he wondered what it was costing him and Imogen.

TRIPLE WORD SCORE

M-E-L.

No, that wouldn't work. *L-E-M.* He looked at his remaining letters. An *N* but no *O.* He clenched his fists as the letters ran together in front of him. He couldn't concentrate. Especially not with Imogen talking to fill the silences between him and Mom.

How quickly things could change. One minute Mom was alive. The next she wasn't. One minute he was thrilled to see her again. And the next—he was weirded out and didn't know what to think.

"*M-E-N,*" Charlie said, laying his tiles on the board. What a lame next move.

"Ooh, good word, Charlie!" Imogen said brightly. Her voice sounded fake. It wasn't a good word. "Five points!"

Charlie wished he had enough letters to play the words he really wanted to.

CONFUSED. Fourteen points.

FREAKED. Fifteen points.

WHAT THE HECK IS GOING ON? Ninety million points. Triple word score. Win the whole game.

"Oops," Imogen said. A broken pencil point sat on the notepad. "I'll go get a new one. I know where they are." She laughed a little. "This is our house, after all." She started to stand when Mom jumped up instead.

"No, you don't need to!" she said in a rush. "You both sit."

"No really, Mom," Imogen said, grabbing onto Mom's arm and not letting go. "I'm happy to. Or we could go together!"

Imogen started to stand up again, but Mom shook her hand away. "No, I'll go get it." Mom's voice was tinged with something that Charlie couldn't quite recognize. He thought it was strange that she was so insistent about getting a pencil.

"Don't leave me again," Imogen whispered. She had a wild look in her eye. Mom was out of the room by the time Imogen finally put her reaching arms down.

Charlie had to take advantage of this moment to talk to Imogen alone.

Before he could say anything, Imogen sighed like she had just eaten the best piece of cake ever. "Isn't this the best, Charlie? Mom's cooking. Scrabble after dinner. Scavenger hunts. This is what I wanted: us all together again."

Charlie looked around and lowered his voice. "Something about this place is off. Did you see the pictures in the hall? Dad's not in any of them."

Imogen pursed her lips and shook her head. "No way. You must have missed him."

"Missed Dad? In every single picture? I don't think so." How could Imogen even think that?

Charlie continued, "And the pictures of us are strange, too. Like parts of us are being erased."

"I think you're seeing things." Imogen had an answer for everything. His words weren't getting through. She wasn't listening.

"And did you see the kind of weird looks that Mom's been giving me? I think she knows that I suspect something."

"Well, you didn't look very happy about hugging her before," Imogen replied. "What's wrong with you? Mom is back and it's the greatest thing ever."

Charlie glanced at the door again. Still no Mom. "Maybe if you take everything alone it doesn't add up to much, but together, don't you think it's kind of weird? She cooks for us, but she hasn't eaten with us. Not a single bite."

"She ate beforehand."

Charlie focused on the scratchiness of the carpet underneath his palms and the way the letter tiles lined up just so on the little wooden game racks. "You're different now. Up there. Down here. Something's changed." His voice gained momentum. "And you put all that with the pictures and the looks and *the fact that we traveled through a hole in your bedroom floor to get to an alternate world or whatever where Mom is alive...*"

At this point, Charlie felt like he was going to erupt. He took a deep breath to settle his heart, which threatened to thump out of his chest. "I just think something's wrong down here."

Imogen's lip trembled. "No, *you're* wrong, Charlie! You are wrong. Mom is here, and things are better than I even remember. They're perfect. It's like Mom never even went away."

"But she—" Charlie said softly.

Imogen shook her head as if to block out his voice, and then looked at him, her eyes burning. "Don't ruin this," she practically spat. "This is all I've wanted!"

Charlie knew, now, that he had gone too far. He shouldn't have told Imogen everything at once. He should have broken it to her better. He could have shown her the pictures in the hall, made her see. Maybe that was why Mom had been so insistent—she didn't want Imogen looking around.

But instead, Imogen sat on the floor, arms crossed over her chest.

He heard a noise behind him; he turned to look. Mom stood in the doorway. Charlie felt his insides deflate like the air being released from a balloon in one giant whoosh. How much had Mom heard?

"I've found one!" Mom crowed, waving a pencil in the air. She sat back down on the carpet. "Ooh, and I've got a word, too."

"M-O-T-H-E-R," she said, using the last of her tiles. "Eleven points. And a triple word score!"

"Yay, Mom!" Imogen cheered, shooting one last glance at Charlie. She added up the scores on the notepad, then subtracted out the tiles she and Charlie still had left. "And you have the highest score!"

"I win!" Mom said, a satisfied smile on her face.

OUT OF BALANCE

Someone was shaking Charlie's shoulder. "Charlie, Charlie, wake up."

Charlie rubbed the sleep from his eyes, the figure before him coming into focus. "Dad, what are you doing in here?" He squinted at the clock on his nightstand and rolled back over. "It's midnight."

"It's noon." Dad pulled up the blinds on the windows, allowing sunlight to stream into the room. It made Charlie's eyes hurt. "You and Imogen both—what's gotten into you? Do you feel okay?"

Dad leaned over and put his hand on Charlie's forehead, just like Mom used to.

"No fever," Dad said. "Maybe I should call Dr. Tortora, just in case."

"We're fine," Charlie said, pasting on a smile even though it hurt to do so. "Just a long week." Under the blanket, he wriggled his fingers and toes. Then his arms and his legs. They were heavy and hard to lift, like they had been filled with sand.

"All right." Dad scrunched up his forehead. Charlie recognized the look. He had seen it a lot on Dad's face when Mom was sick: he was worried. "I just want to make sure you're okay." A lump formed at the back of Charlie's throat. He nodded.

"I've got to get a little work done today. But there's some leftover pizza in the fridge that you guys could split." He paused. "I'll try not to be gone too long." Charlie nodded again. He didn't trust his voice. He tried to push the thought of Dad eating alone in front of the TV out of his mind.

Charlie listened until he heard the garage door close and leaned back on his pillow with a groan. Again his head felt like someone had been playing very loud drum music in his ears all night. He tried to keep his head very still as he turned over on his side. When he did, a paper crinkled underneath him. Moving very slowly, he pulled it out, unfolded it, and smoothed out the wrinkles. It was dated with yesterday's date and a time: 5:20 p.m.

SCRABBLE WITH MOM

- *At hospital.*
- *Camping trip. Raccoon attack—lost X tile.*
- *Friday nights with pizza.*

It was Charlie's handwriting. He remembered writing it and tucking it into the pocket of his jeans—the jeans he was still wearing—before they went down the hatch last night. Imogen had told him to hurry up, so the last two were sort of scrawled, but he could still read them.

But it might as well have been someone else who wrote them, because he couldn't remember any of those times. What he held in his hand now, though, was proof. Before, when he had talked to Elliott about the spaghetti, he had suspected things, but it was hard to prove you were losing your memories when you couldn't remember what they were in the first place. This piece of paper, though, proved it.

Maybe Imogen would believe him now.

Charlie's stomach rumbled. He shoved on some slippers, padded into the kitchen, and pulled the pizza box out of the fridge. He didn't bother heating it up and jumped up on the counter stool. The answering machine light blinked; taking a bite, he pushed the button.

"Hey, Charlie—it's Rohan. Where are you? We're at school waiting for you. Remember we were supposed to practice

today. Mathletes? Mr. Spencer even brought doughnuts. I've had seven so far. Get here when you can. We need you."

Charlie's heart sank right down to the bottom of the soles of his feet. He had missed the extra practice. He forgot and slept right through it. He remembered talking to Rohan about it last Tuesday. Mr. Spencer had set it up special; it was the only day he could get the gym. The team was going to do a practice round on the stage with buzzers and everything.

The machine continued playing. *"Where are you, Charlie?"*

It was Miranda, and she sounded mad.

"You're already twenty minutes late. Rohan ate all the glazed doughnuts and only left me jelly filled. I know that's not your fault, but it kind of feels like it is."

There was a scuffle at the other end and a yelp. Then June came on.

"If you don't come soon, you won't get a say in the T-shirts."

Miranda yelled in the background. *"Good! He doesn't deserve one."*

The call ended. There were no more messages.

Charlie thought about throwing on a clean shirt and riding his bike up to school, but glancing at the clock, he realized they were done an hour or so ago. So instead, he opened the trash can and threw the rest of his pizza away. He had lost his appetite.

Mom had said that you could only be in one place at a time—this world or the other. But Charlie was finding that wasn't exactly true. The worlds seemed to be spilling out into each other, mixing together and making a giant mess of both.

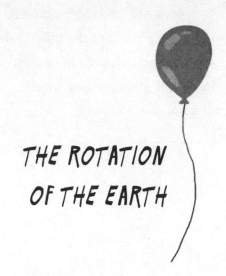

THE ROTATION
OF THE EARTH

*T*ime began to blend together for Charlie. One hour into the next. Sunday night, Dad didn't ask if they wanted to have dinner together, which made Charlie want to rewind time and say yes to Dad's pizza. And actually show up at Mathletes practice so he didn't feel like he was letting himself and everyone else down.

Instead, he and Imogen went down to see Mom again. They had a dance party in the middle of the living room and started on a five-hundred-piece puzzle of the Golden Gate Bridge and ate ice cream sundaes complete with rainbow sprinkles. They talked about things they had done in the past, too. Mom loved hearing about their old times together, she said.

Charlie started to keep a list of memories he was losing on a sheet of loose-leaf. He found himself studying these instead of the invertebrates, thinking that maybe if he closed his eyes a little tighter, he might be able to force the memories out.

It didn't work.

What it did do was make Charlie late to school. Dad had pounded on his door and Imogen's around eight thirty Monday morning, saying, "You're late for school, you're late for school!" like he was some kind of town crier that Charlie had read about in his social studies textbook.

With five minutes to get ready, Charlie splashed some water on his face in the bathroom to try to wake up. He splattered some on the mirror, and when he went to wipe it off, he really looked at himself for the first time since this all began.

What he saw made him jump back and then look harder.

He looked like Imogen had the morning of her birthday, after she'd seen Mom for the first time—hair askew, kind of vacant look, puffy face, bruised eyes.

He looked like Frank before he disappeared.

Charlie made it to school just as the second-period bell rang. Dad had dropped them both off—Imogen first and Charlie second. Right as he was getting out of the car, Dad grabbed his arm. "Are you sure everything's okay? Is it school? Your friends?"

Charlie just shook his head. "I'm good. Thanks for the ride." In response, Dad held on to him a second or two longer.

At his locker, Charlie opened his book bag to unpack his stuff and groaned. In his hurry that morning, he had totally forgotten to pack his lunch. And Dad hadn't given him any money to buy something in the cafeteria. The wrong kind of bread tasted better than nothing at all.

He rested his head on the cool metal of the locker, resisting the urge to smash his fist into it. Then came a gentle touch on his shoulder.

"Charlie!"

He turned. A flush-faced Elliott stood in front of him.

"I called you last night—after I got home from the campout. I wanted to see if you wanted to study for our science test."

Charlie's stomach began to churn—a mixture of hunger and the anxious feeling that this day was going to be full of these moments.

"Did you get my message?"

He shook his head.

"I was calling your name all the way down the hall. It was like you didn't hear me. In the zone, I guess, or something."

She laughed, but her voice was strained. Concern washed over her face. She reached out and put her hand against his forehead. "Are you sick or something? You look kind of terrible right now."

If only she knew. He looked terrible. He felt terrible. He wasn't sure how much longer he could keep this up. He shook his head. "I'm okay."

He wasn't.

"Umm." She tilted her head to the side, waiting. When it became clear that Charlie wasn't going to say anything else, she continued, "So I ran into Dr. Miller in the hallway this morning before homeroom, and remember how I said that the balloons weren't as bad as the grief picnic?"

Charlie nodded.

"Well, we're going to release the balloons at a grief picnic. In Tiny Meadows. On Friday."

Charlie started to shake his head, but Elliott kept talking.

"And I know grief group's not really your thing. And that's okay, but there'll be hot dogs and hamburgers and I know you really like those—that's a plus, right? And if you have food in your mouth, you won't have to talk. So there's that." Elliott looked at her shoes. "I'd also like it if you were there."

Almost every part of Charlie wanted to say no. He didn't want the talking about your feelings or the thinking about your feelings or really anything to do with feelings—even if they did come with cookout food.

He raked his hands through his hair and let out a breath.

Elliott took a step back. "Did I say something wrong? I mean, if you don't want to go, that's okay—"

"Oh no, no," Charlie said. "That's not what I meant. I just don't know—I'll go."

"Really?"

Charlie shoved his hands in his pockets. "Yeah, it will be fun, right?"

Elliott broke into a giant grin. "Great! Oh and Dr. Miller wanted us to partner up for things—you know decorations, food, activities. . . ."

Charlie groaned inwardly. He hadn't known there was work involved. Besides, if the balloon thing was any indication, the activities at the picnic were going to be lame.

"And I told her I'd be your partner. You know, if you were coming." She paused for a beat as if gauging how to finish her thought. "I volunteered us for decorations! I have extra paint and stuff from Pep Squad. So I thought we could meet tonight and plan. My house at seven, okay?"

Charlie nodded, mentally thinking about how he could stall Imogen for a few hours. He didn't want her going down to visit Mom alone.

Elliott glanced at the clock on the wall. "Ooh. I have to

go. We have an emergency Science Olympiad meeting. You know scientists. I'll see you tonight."

"I'll be there." It was as much a promise to Elliott as it was to himself.

For Charlie it was as if the rotation of the earth had picked up speed and he was losing his grip—on Dad, on Imogen, on Mathletes, on everything he loved. One false move, one little slip, and Charlie felt he'd lose his balance and go flying out into space. And he couldn't help but think that the one difference, the one change, was seeing Mom again.

BAD TO WORSE

*E*very time Charlie sat down in science, June would turn around before class and say, "Did you know . . ." followed by some crazy, almost unbelievable fact about things like wombat mating rituals or the strength of human hair. June remembered most everything she heard, which was why she was so great on Mathletes and on Science Olympiad with Elliott.

But it also meant she didn't forget things easily. Or forgive. Which was why, Charlie guessed, she didn't turn around that Monday.

"Did you know . . . ," Charlie began to the back of June's hair. She leaned back slightly. He could tell she was listening.

". . . that I really did forget about Mathletes? And I'm really sorry."

June turned around and peered at him through her large, dark-framed glasses. On anyone else, they would have looked ridiculous, but June made them look really cool. "Okay, I believe you," she said. "But you still didn't get a vote on shirts."

"What did you pick?" he asked.

"Miranda's idea," she said. "And I got to pick the color— orange. So Rohan's pretty upset—about you and the shirts."

Charlie winced. "Thanks for the heads-up." He had already guessed that based on the messages and also the fact that he hadn't called Rohan back last night at all to explain. Because he had been with Mom.

June scanned him up and down. "You look awful, by the way. No offense."

"None taken, I guess."

"Maybe you aren't getting enough sleep," she said. "Did you know that you need at least eight and a half hours a night? That's what I tell my auntie at least when she tries to wake me up at seven. Science, right?"

Charlie stifled the urge to laugh because if he started, he wasn't sure that he would stop. Eight and a half hours a night? Right now, he was averaging about three.

The bell rang and Mrs. Looper flicked the lights on and

off. June turned back around.

"All right, scientists," she said. "Ready or not, and you better be ready—" She scanned the class, her eyes squinted. Charlie was pretty sure they settled on him. But maybe he was just feeling guilty. "We're taking our science test. Pencils out, books and papers away, you have forty-five minutes. Take your time, check your work, et cetera, et cetera."

Mrs. Looper handed a pile of tests out to each row. June handed him one over her shoulder, and he began to skim. With every question he read, his heart beat faster, faster. The words blurred in front of his eyes. Sure there were a few he could answer from paying attention in class, but for most of these, he only had guesses.

At the end of forty-five minutes, Charlie stared at his test. He had never done this terribly. It wasn't the kind of fake terrible where he'd tell Miranda he'd done awful on the math test and then get an A. This was legitimate failing. He had only answered tén questions and hadn't even done any of the extended responses.

When he handed the test to Mrs. Looper, she kind of shook her head and put her hand on his back. "Let's talk about this tomorrow, Charlie," she said, and moved down the row.

Charlie wasn't sure how this day could get any worse.

* * *

Charlie knew he needed to talk to Rohan, but he couldn't hang around at the end of the day. He had to get Imogen from play practice. When he opened the gym door to her school, though, he saw another girl he didn't recognize in Imogen's ruby slippers. He watched for a moment; the new Dorothy stumbled around the stage, missing lines and speaking out of turn. Charlie sighed. He didn't even stop to ask Mrs. Talley where Imogen was. He knew. She had quit the play, just like she said she was going to. He stepped back out into the cool autumn air and closed the door behind him.

Imogen was lying on her bed when he got home.

She didn't move when he opened her door and stepped into her room.

"Imogen?" he said, taking another step toward her. Her bed was still pushed to the side from the first time Charlie had moved it, and the door to the hatch was open, waiting. Even though he had so many uncertainties about Mom and that other world, he was still drawn to it.

He closed his eyes and counted to ten, balling up his hands at his side, resisting the pull of the hatch.

"Imogen?" he tried again.

"Is it time to go back down yet?" It was the only question Imogen asked anymore.

"Why did you quit the play?" Charlie answered instead.

Imogen didn't speak for a moment, and Charlie could

feel the distance between them growing bigger.

"Mom can't be there. Only the things I do with Mom matter anymore."

Imogen's words sucked all the wind out of Charlie, as if he had been hit in the gut.

"But you love acting." What he really wanted to say was, *What about me? What about Dad?*

"I did. But it's not important anymore."

"But what's Dad going to say?"

"I don't know, Charlie. Maybe he can write it on a Post-it."

"What about Lily? What about Min? What about your other friends?"

Imogen didn't answer this. She only turned over in her bed so that her back was to Charlie. "Is it time to go down yet?"

Charlie was torn. On one hand, he didn't want to leave Imogen here alone and chance that she'd visit Mom by herself. On the other, he had promised Elliott that they would make decorations together. And after letting down Rohan and the other Mathletes, his science teacher, and himself, he couldn't disappoint Elliott, too.

"I have to go over to Elliott's," Charlie said. "We're working on a project together. Dad will be home soon to make some dinner. I want you to wait for me, Imogen."

"I can't promise that," she said.

Two giant leaps across the room and Charlie was standing over Imogen's bed, his fingers circled around her wrist. His hand was shaking.

"Imogen, please," he said.

Imogen tried to pull away. "Stop, Charlie. You're hurting me." Charlie dropped her hand, looking in horror at the red imprints his fingers had made.

"I'm sorry, I'm sorry." Charlie was losing his balance. He couldn't control what was going on in this world or the other. The world spun even faster than before. This whole thing was turning him into some kind of monster.

Imogen cradled her wrist in her hand. "I'll wait for you," she whispered.

CONSTELLATIONS

Charlie stood on Elliott's porch for what seemed like forever. He couldn't seem to stop his hands from shaking. His finger hovered over the doorbell. Finally, he pressed down and waited, counting the beats from the time he heard the sound of the chime to the second someone opened the door, so his mind could focus on something, anything, besides what had happened with Imogen.

"Charlie!" a voice exclaimed from the other side of the door, seven and a half seconds later. The lock clicked, the door opened, and Mrs. Roberts pulled him into a hug as Charlie's arms hung at his side. He normally worked to avoid these attack hugs, but this time he let himself fall into it. It was a little bit comforting to know that something was real.

When Mrs. Roberts pulled back, she held him at arm's length. "How are you?"

How was he? He shifted his weight to his back leg and lowered his gaze. Mrs. Roberts was giving him the kind of look Mom used to when she knew something was wrong. "I'm okay," he stammered.

"Mom!" Fingers circled Charlie's arm and pulled him out of Mrs. Roberts's grasp. "Decorations wait for no one!" Elliott had scissors and glue and stickers and other stuff Charlie couldn't even identify in her hands.

Elliott's mom sighed. "Is this something else you signed up for? We talked about this, between cross-country and Science Olympiad, I just don't think this is healthy. . . ."

Elliott sighed back. "No, we were asked to do this. For the *grief* group. See, processing! Talking! Healing!" She threw the words over her shoulder as she marched Charlie up the stairs. When they got to her room, Elliott fumbled with the doorknob, and her face flushed red.

Charlie reached out and put his hand over hers, turning the knob.

"Sorry," Elliott said, pulling her hand away. She tugged nervously at her ponytail. "She just wants to talk about feelings all the time, and sometimes I just need some space. You know?"

Without thinking, Charlie blurted, "My dad never wants to talk." The moment it was out, he regretted it. He had told Elliott a lot—more than most people, but still. It was the most he had said in a very long time, and it felt like he was exposing a little bit of himself, the part he had hidden away.

He tensed his shoulders, expecting Elliott to ask him questions and want to talk more about it and why he was late to school today and why he couldn't seem to stop shaking. But she didn't.

Instead, she nodded and handed him a scissors. His muscles relaxed. Elliott always seemed to understand him.

"So, what kind of theme do you want to do? I pulled up some ideas on my computer," she said, grabbing the laptop on her desk and flopping down on her beanbag chair. Charlie's line of sight went directly to the picture frame on the desk—Elliott and her brother making fish faces at the camera. He recognized it from the newspaper articles.

Elliott caught him staring. "Mom wanted to put in the picture of us at Jack's First Communion, but Jack hated that suit. And my dress was some heinous flower print, so—"

"I like this one," Charlie said. They looked so happy in it.

"I do, too." Elliott smiled sadly. "It was from that morning. We were supposed to go to the zoo." She then shook her head and sat on the floor, folding her impossibly long legs into a pretzel shape. Charlie sat down next to her and looked over her shoulder as she clicked on the different websites. Elliott went on about animals and cupcakes and balloon themes.

She clicked through some different pictures. "So what do you think about this one?" Elliott pointed at a star theme. Bright Christmas lights encircled a picnic area, and strung up between trees were stars of all different shapes and colors. There were bright starbursts coming out of a tin can in the center of the tables, which were covered in tablecloths decorated with constellations.

Charlie was not really into decorating, but this was a theme he could go for.

"That looks cool," he said, but then paused. "But won't it still be daylight? The lights won't show up then."

Elliott shook her head. "Dr. Miller reserved the park shelter from five to seven. So it won't be really dark, but it might be dark enough."

Then a memory returned, one he had tucked away in the back of his mind.

"Is it dark enough, Mom?" Imogen had asked.

Mom only grinned and flipped off the lights. Even though they knew what was coming next, Imogen and Charlie still held their breath in anticipation.

Then, as if the sky had exploded, giant constellations appeared on the wall across from Imogen's bed where they sat. One after another after another.

Imogen oohed and aahed and clapped her hands with every single constellation. It was like Mom had harnessed the magic of the stars. Their own private viewing of the night sky.

Charlie hadn't seen Imogen that excited in a very long time. Maybe he and Imogen could do that again with Mom. Maybe tonight when they went down again to see her. "Hey, do you have a flashlight and a black piece of paper?"

Elliott nodded, popped up, and retrieved them from her desk.

Carefully, Charlie traced a circle on the paper and cut it out. Using the scissors, he punched a shape into the circle and positioned it in front of the light. "Okay, now turn the lights off."

Elliott did, and Charlie shone the light against the wall of her room. A constellation appeared. Just like he remembered.

"That's amazing," Elliott exclaimed. She reached out as if to touch it. "Which constellation is that?"

"Draco—the dragon." He went to the window, and Elliott followed. Charlie placed his hands against the glass, cupping them around his eyes. "It's still too light out, but later, if you look north, you'll see it. Right there!" He pointed to a spot in the sky. He wished they could see it for real now.

"Awesome," Elliott breathed. "How'd they get their names?"

Charlie shrugged. "Mom said that most come from the Greeks. They'd make up these stories about the night sky to keep themselves entertained. They linked them up to things they knew, like Leo, the lion, and then some of them came from modern astronomers."

"Have you ever wanted to name one?" Elliott asked.

"Sometimes," Charlie said. "When we'd go out to the country to see them, Mom and Imogen would name some. Like, Imogen named one after a starfish she found on the beach. But I'm waiting till I find something perfect."

"And then you could make one of these star cards for it," Elliott said. "How'd you learn to make these?"

"When Mom got sick and she couldn't drive us out to the country anymore, she said she'd bring the stars to us." The stacks and stacks of constellation cards that Mom had made were shoved underneath his bed—forgotten and dusty. "I have some of these that we can use if you think they'll work."

"Definitely," Elliott said. Her head tilted to the side as if studying him, and her mouth bent up into a half smile. It was an expression that Charlie couldn't quite read, but he thought it looked like a promise.

"Well, this will be the best grief picnic ever," Charlie said. "At least the best decorated."

Elliott laughed, and that made Charlie smile.

A BOY AND HIS DOG

Charlie had just pulled his jacket tighter and was half-way home when he heard her. The jingle of tags, her uneven gallop because her left side didn't move quite as fast as her right, her huffs and puffs. They were some of Charlie's favorite sounds in the world.

He turned and Ruby plowed him over right there on the sidewalk, nearly knocking him out of his sneakers. He couldn't believe how happy he was to see her. He buried his hands underneath her fur as she licked his face. "What are you doing out again?"

Ruby barked in response and danced around him, her toenails clicking.

146

Charlie laughed. "I think that Edna needs a better gate or something." Still, he nestled up next to her, putting his arm around her back. They sat there together on the sidewalk, the only light coming from the streetlamps that lined the road and the stars that stretched out above them.

After a few moments of quiet, Charlie said, "Have you ever not known what to do?" The question had been bumping around in his brain the entire walk home.

Ruby's cheeks puffed out, hot air landing on Charlie's cheek.

"Okay. Or maybe you know what you *should* do, but you kind of don't want to do it." He knew he should try to convince Imogen that they shouldn't go to the other world that night. "Something's not right down there, but I still want to see Mom. Is that crazy?" It sounded even crazier when he said it out loud.

Ruby barked.

"I know. I know it is." He scratched her behind her ears. "There was this one time, when I was seven. I found the Halloween candy hidden under a pile of coats in the closet. I was only going to take a piece, but it was so good. So I took another and another."

Ruby groaned, burying her head into his shoulder. "And after a while, I was sticky and covered in chocolate and felt like I was going to throw up, but I just kept eating the candy.

That's what this other world is like."

"Just one more visit, Ruby," Charlie said. Ruby whined and seemed agitated. "We'll just go one more time and then we'll be done with it." He wasn't quite sure who he was trying to convince—Ruby or himself.

He sat with Ruby for a long time, even though it was windy and cold and his legs were numb and wet from the sidewalk. He just couldn't seem to let go of her. She was one thing that still made him feel firmly rooted in the real world.

STRANGE OBJECTS
IN THE SKY

*C*harlie's attempts to convince Imogen not to go visit Mom were halfhearted at best. Even his conversation with Ruby wasn't enough to stop him from visiting Mom again. He didn't have the willpower to stay away, and most of all, he wanted Mom back in their lives, too. Hope was a powerful thing.

He and Imogen waited until the footsteps upstairs had stilled and they were certain Dad was in bed before opening the hatch. This time, Mom wasn't waiting with dinner on the table.

"I had a different idea," Mom said. "There's always time for eating. I thought we could do some of your favorite

149

things! All together again."

Imogen grabbed Mom's hand and cheered. "Yes! I've been writing down everything I want to do with you now. I have a list!"

Charlie forced a grin. He knew the catch.

Mom leveled her gaze at Charlie. "Charlie first! What do you want to do?"

He thought for a moment. He'd have to pick something that he didn't care if he lost. He wanted to hold on to every memory.

"The stars," Imogen said. "Your telescope!"

Charlie's stomach sank. Not the stars, not his telescope. Those memories were too important. He started to say no, but then he saw a strange look pass over Mom.

"Oh, I don't think Charlie wants to do that yet," she said hurriedly. "There are so many other things that we could all do."

"But it would be so fun," Imogen said. "Remember my starfish constellation and all the sky stories you would tell?"

Charlie watched Mom carefully. She bent down next to Imogen; her smile was barely a smile. "Of course, but this is Charlie's choice, and it seems like he wants to choose something else."

Charlie wasn't going to say no now. When Mom had been so adamant about the pencil during the Scrabble game, he was certain it was because she didn't want Imogen looking around. Maybe the telescope or something held more clues about what this place was.

"Great idea," Charlie said. "We haven't done that in so long! Let's go!"

Before Mom could move to suggest anything else, Charlie pushed past her and Imogen and into his room. Even though he had been down here several times, he had never been in his room before. Like Imogen's, it looked exactly the same as the world above—just cleaner and neater and unlived in—with everything put in its proper place. That was how Charlie knew that his star map was in the upper right-hand drawer of his desk and the telescope was tucked away in the closet.

He pulled out the telescope, holding it and the tripod in one hand and the star map in the other. The room was still dark since he hadn't flipped on the light, but his eyes adjusted. Besides, he had set up the telescope a thousand times before. It had become automatic.

Imogen and Mom sat on Charlie's bed and watched as he finished turning the gears and dials on the telescope.

"We could do something else, Charlie," Mom said. There was a hitch in her voice, but Charlie wouldn't be dissuaded. He hadn't found anything in the closet. There had been clothes, his hamper, his old sleeping bag from camp, the monster movie marathon poster he and Frank had gotten from the local theater. The clue had to be elsewhere.

"This is what I want to do." Charlie spread out the star map on the floor. There was still a little light—from the streetlamps outside and the star stickers on his ceiling—so he could make out the constellations and their locations.

But Charlie didn't look into the eyepiece of the telescope—not yet. Telescopes zoomed so close up that they only showed a portion of a constellation. He wanted to see the whole thing. He grabbed a pair of binoculars that was sitting on the top of his dresser and looked out to the night sky. The skies were easier to see in this world because there wasn't the light from other houses or buildings to pollute the dark.

Charlie started with Andromeda. Then he scanned over to the Big Dipper. He focused on one star after another after another until the pain in his head and neck started again. He stopped on one in particular and focused on the pain as it grew, spreading out farther and farther. He imagined it traveling through his veins and nerve endings. Then, right before his eyes, just as the pain in his head was at its worst, the star he was looking at disappeared.

It couldn't have. Charlie knew that stars had a life span—just like humans. They were born and then millions and millions of years later, they died. But that star just winked out. It wasn't supposed to work like that.

Charlie let the binoculars go loose against the lanyard around his neck and held up the star map. He worked to match up each of the stars to their appropriate spots in the sky. The star he just watched disappear wasn't the only one missing.

He turned back to Mom and Imogen. "Can I look now, Charlie?" Imogen asked. "Is it my turn?" She kicked her feet against the side of the bed.

"There are stars missing," Charlie said. "From the sky. That's not supposed to happen. I just saw one disappear." He got louder with every word. It felt like everything was wrong and out of whack and *spinning, spinning, spinning* in his brain.

"You must be reading the map wrong," Imogen said, looking at him, then Mom, then back to him.

"I am not reading the map wrong," Charlie insisted. "I am not reading the map wrong. Look for yourself." He threw the map toward them and spun around to face the window.

He couldn't believe what he saw next. Charlie flew to the windowsill and pressed his face against the glass to get a closer look. There was a boy walking down the street with someone else. Charlie fumbled with the binoculars, finally grabbing hold of them. He smashed them against his eyes, almost poking one with the eyepiece.

But he could see more clearly now, especially as the boy

walked under one of the streetlamps. Charlie recognized the spiky black hair and the untied shoes. Then he recognized the person the boy was walking with—Grandma. "Frank!" Charlie screamed. "Frank!" The boy didn't look up.

Charlie tried to unlatch the window and push up on it. One, two, three times. The window wouldn't budge. So he turned on his heel and raced out the bedroom door, narrowly missing Mom's outstretched hands and ignoring Imogen's confused cries.

He unlocked the front door and stumbled out onto the porch, his chest heaving. He looked to the left and then to the right. The street was empty again.

"Frank!" Charlie yelled, sinking to his knees.

He'd seen Frank—Frank who had been missing. Frank who he hadn't seen in months. This Frank wasn't wearing his favorite gray cap, but still Charlie was sure it had been him. Just like he was certain he'd seen a star disappear from the sky. A star that disappeared just as he got that headache. Just as he couldn't remember any other times that he had looked at the stars with Mom.

Imogen. He had to get Imogen out now.

Charlie hopped to his feet and ran back into the house.

Mom and Imogen were waiting in the family room. Charlie grabbed Imogen's arm and tried to pull her to her room so they could enter the hatch and go back to the real world. He needed Imogen to be safe.

"What are you doing?" Imogen asked, yanking her arm back. Her eyes were big. "I don't want to go."

"Please, Imogen," Charlie pleaded. "It's not safe here for us. Frank's here. He's maybe been here the whole time. We could go missing, too."

Imogen grabbed Mom and clung onto her waist. "No, Charlie. I'm not going anywhere. I want to stay here forever."

FOREVER

The words echoed in Charlie's head. *I want to stay here forever.*

Mom had stood there quietly this whole time, a little smile on her face, but at Imogen's words, she leaned in. "Oh, that would be wonderful," she said slowly, as if she were considering the idea. "I've missed you so much, Imogen!" She put her hand on Imogen's head. Imogen only held on to Mom's waist tighter.

Another alarm sounded in Charlie's head. There was nothing right about this. Before Mom had died, she had asked Charlie and Imogen to take care of Dad and to take care of each other. She wouldn't want to separate them. She wouldn't want them to leave Dad and everything else they loved forever.

Charlie mustered up every bit of courage he had and said, "You are not Mom."

"Charlie!" Imogen said. "That is not very nice. Of course it's Mom."

Mom ignored his accusation. "I'd love for you to stay down here, too, Charlie. We can all be one happy family again."

Charlie shot forward. "NO!" He grabbed Imogen's other hand and pulled her up, away from Mom. Imogen tried to yank her arm away again, but Charlie held tight. "Something is going on here that is not normal, and we need to get out."

"But what about our memories, Charlie?" Mom took a step toward him. "Don't you want to relive them here with me?"

"I do!" Imogen said. She reared back and kicked Charlie in the shin. Charlie stumbled back but managed to keep a grip on her arm. Imogen bucked like a wild pony. "You're hurting me, Charlie!" she said through gritted teeth.

He pulled her out of the family room. Her heels dragged on the carpet, and she let her body go limp. Man, she was heavy when she wanted to be.

"Charlie?" Mom tried again.

For a moment, Charlie stopped. He loved Mom. He missed Mom. But then his gaze settled on the hallway. And the pictures. And everything this world had subtracted out.

On the hardest problem of his life, Charlie was finally ready to buzz in. Mom was trying to subtract Imogen and Charlie out from the real world.

She must have seen something change in his face, because her mouth became a thin line and her eyes narrowed and now Mom didn't even look like Mom anymore.

Imogen's fists continued to rain down on his chest, and he braced himself for another kick to the shin. "I'm not going with you!" Mom now stood in the corner watching them, arms folded over her chest, silent.

"Imogen, please," he said. Beads of sweat formed across his brow. "We have to go now."

For a second, he wondered why this was so easy. Sure, he'd have nasty black-and-blue marks down his legs tomorrow morning, but Imogen was the only one putting up a fight. He'd have to think about it later. Right now, he had to get her out.

His hand encircled the doorknob of Imogen's bedroom just as her fist connected with his ear. His head vibrated like a struck bell. The only relief came from the fact that the hatch was near. Keeping one arm around Imogen, he braced the other on the door and summoned all his strength to pull both of them into her room and down into the hatch.

"I'll be back, Mom! I promise!" Imogen yelled.

Charlie slammed the door shut over the top of them, but right before it closed, he heard Mom say, "I know."

ACCUSATIONS

*I*mogen wouldn't leave the hatch in the real world. So Charlie had to grab hold of her sneakers while avoiding her kicks and lift her up and over the edge. He wanted to collapse on the floor. His arms hurt and his brain hurt and his heart hurt. But he couldn't be done yet. Not when he knew the danger that he and Imogen faced from the other world.

He pulled Imogen into the garage. He couldn't leave her in the room alone or else she'd go straight back down to Mom. She had gone with him somewhat quietly, which unnerved him. "Why are we in here?" she asked. Her voice was blank, scary.

When he grabbed a box of nails and a hammer from the workbench, her eyes flashed with sudden recognition. "Charlie, no!"

He didn't say anything and instead ran for the bedroom. She chased after him, scratching at his arms and pulling at his legs. He shrugged her off and grabbed a nail from the box. He fell to the floor and, positioning the nail, began to drive it into the wood. Imogen would understand later. She'd have to. This was the right thing to do.

Pieces of wood splintered off as he hammered. He put one in his pocket. He had to remind himself that this was real.

"You can't do this!" Imogen wailed, trying to stop the hammer mid-swing. "Mom's down there. You don't love her anymore, Charlie. You've forgotten about her."

The accusations hit Charlie square in the chest. He did love Mom. He did trust Mom. But what he knew about *this* Mom scared him. This wasn't Real Mom, the one they remembered, the one they loved. This was some Mom replacement, some Not-Mom who stole their memories and wanted them to leave this world forever.

And Frank. Frank was down there. The thought almost made Charlie stop hammering. He couldn't leave him there. But he didn't want Imogen to disappear, too. Right now, all he could do was keep her safe.

Charlie pounded in another nail. And between every pound he held his breath, waiting, hoping that Dad would hear it. Or hear Imogen's yelling or the kicks she landed on his legs. That he'd storm in and ask what was going on.

But Dad never came.

By the time Charlie had the door sealed as best he could, Imogen had crumpled into a tired heap in the corner of her room. Her face was blotchy red and her hands were flat against the hardwood as if at any moment, she might try to peel the boards up.

Charlie wanted to curl up just like Imogen. His arms and head felt heavy. His shoulders were practically hunched up to his ears, and his eyes blurred what was in front of him, like he was seeing things underwater. But there was still more he had to do. He stood and braced himself against the bed once again. It hadn't been so long ago that he was moving it away from the hatch. Now, he was moving it back.

The bed's legs loudly scratched across the bedroom floor, though his noodly arms could barely budge the bed an inch. Turning around, so that his back was against the mattress, he pushed and pushed until the bed was finally in place, centered directly over the small door.

Charlie collapsed onto the bed with a groan and stuck an aching arm behind him to grab one of Imogen's pillows. He tucked it under his head. He clutched the hammer to him as if it were a stuffed bear and flipped over. He kept one eye on Imogen and one eye on the hatch.

He'd stay here tonight. Because even with the nails and the bed and the hammer, it didn't quite seem like enough to protect Imogen.

And as he drifted off to sleep, Mom's voice still echoed.

I know. I know. I know.

THE HEALING
HEARTS PICNIC

At school the next day, Charlie ended up in the very last place he thought he'd ever go on a voluntary basis.

Dr. Miller's office.

He paused outside the door for a moment. It was almost all the way open, but Dr. Miller didn't seem to notice him as she sat hunched over her keyboard, typing furiously. Her messy hair was thrown into a bun, which bobbed up and down as she typed. The pencil she could never find was tucked squarely into it.

The room was small. Practically a janitor's closet, minus the cleaning supplies but adding in the "feel good about yourself" junk that cluttered the walls. If Charlie was in charge of making counselors' offices, he would make them huge to allow for the most distance between himself and Dr. Miller as possible.

Dr. Miller said the close space invited Community and Understanding and Compassion. Charlie thought it invited things like Claustrophobia and Unwanted Sharing and Forced Closeness. He also wondered if those were things Dr. Miller told herself to make her feel better about having the smallest office in school, but he didn't have any evidence to back that up.

Charlie decided to knock. It felt more formal, less make yourself at home and get comfortable.

When Dr. Miller looked up from her desk to see who it was, her face lit up in a giant grin. "Charlie!" she called. She smoothed her pants and adjusted her glasses in anticipation. He was surprised she didn't clap her hands. This moment of "seeking help" must be what counselors lived for. At group, Dr. Miller always made these large, exaggerated arm gestures and said, "Let's share ourselves. Let's be OPEN with each other." She must have thought he was going to be OPEN with her. If he was, he'd never get out of counseling.

She closed her laptop lid. "Come in. Come in. You're always welcome."

Charlie pulled his lips up into what he hoped looked like a smile. "Uh, thanks."

Dr. Miller patted the worn yellow chair next to her. "Sit. Sit." She had this odd habit of repeating words and phrases while nodding her head thoughtfully. It might have been a counselor thing.

"So, I had a question," Charlie started. He kept his back straight as a board and hands folded in his lap.

Dr. Miller grabbed her notepad off her desk. If it had been any other time, Charlie would have loved to see what she wrote about him in there. Probably *angry kid, messed up, can't be helped*, but it wasn't another time. He had other stuff to worry about. "It's not that kind of question."

Dr. Miller's face fell a little bit, and she put the notepad back. "Oh. Of course. Of course."

"So, I wondered if I might be able to bring my little sister to the grief picnic on Friday." He tried not to think about how Imogen had ignored him this morning. How she wouldn't even look at him.

"You mean the Healing Hearts picnic, Charlie," she corrected, pointing at the flyer on her bulletin board (next to the dumb smiling flower poster). "Remember, working through our grief will eventually heal our hearts." He could tell from her satisfied smile that Dr. Miller had thought that one up herself.

"Uh, yeah. The Healing Hearts picnic."

All morning, Charlie had gone back and forth about going. He needed to be home for Imogen to keep her safe.

But every time he considered skipping it, he pictured Elliott's disappointed face and her having to hang up all the decorations they'd made by herself. The next best option was bringing Imogen along.

Dr. Miller clapped her hands. "Oh, Charlie, that's a wonderful idea. I only wish I had thought of it myself. Of course she can come." He braced himself for what he knew would follow.

"You know, I feel like this is a little bit of a breakthrough for you."

Charlie nodded, hopeful that if he kept nodding at even intervals, he wouldn't have to say any more. He watched the clock as it ticked by, and Dr. Miller as she gestured with her hands, and waited until she took a breath.

"So, I've got to get to class."

"Oh yes! Absolutely!" She looked at him for an extended moment. Charlie wriggled in his seat. "You're going to be okay, Charlie. I just know it."

He hoped that Dr. Miller was right.

Elliott was waiting outside the office, standing up straight against the hallway wall. Her cheeks flushed when she saw Charlie, and her eyes went to his shoes.

"Umm, hey!"

Charlie nodded, and her face grew even redder.

"So, I was coming to ask Dr. Miller about some things

we'll need for setup and I saw you were in there and so I decided to wait here for you so we could confirm the decorations and stuff and then you were taking a while and I thought leaving would be awkward but staying would also be awkward and I had to make a choice, so here I am! I wasn't listening in or anything."

Normally Charlie would laugh, but he couldn't now. The moment he saw Elliott, the secrets he had been keeping threatened to break free. Each one took up so much space that they stretched his skin thin like a balloon, and it was just a matter of time before he popped.

He had to tell someone besides Ruby about what was going on. Especially about Frank. Imogen was safe now, he hoped, but he couldn't leave Frank down there. Frank had been his best friend. No, Frank was still his best friend.

Charlie looked down the hall to the left and then to the right and then in at Dr. Miller, who watched them curiously through her open door. He motioned for Elliott to follow him, and they tucked themselves away behind a set of lockers. The bell rang and students began to fill the halls, along with the sounds of excited chatter and screams and locker doors opening and slamming shut.

"I have something to tell you," Charlie said. He looked around, making sure that no one was listening in. He pulled Elliott closer and whispered in her ear. "But I can't tell you now. There are too many people around, and I don't have enough time to tell you everything." He paused. "You'll need to hear everything."

When Charlie pulled back, Elliott's face was serious. "What is it? Are you in trouble? Do you need help?"

"Maybe," Charlie started. "Yes, I think I need help."

Saying those words relieved a little bit more of the pressure on his insides.

"Do you want to talk after school?"

Charlie nodded. "But I can't talk at school. I have to leave right when the last bell rings to make sure I'm home for Imogen."

Elliott's eyebrows scrunched. "Doesn't she have play practice? She was running around with that stuffed dog on a leash last week." So much had changed since then, Charlie thought. Last week felt like light-years away.

"She quit."

Elliott didn't say anything for a moment, but her mouth made a tiny O shape.

Finally she spoke: "I'll be there. I'll drop my stuff off at home, and I'll come right over after that."

Charlie's shoulders sagged in relief. He couldn't bear all this alone anymore. He had done this one hard thing— inviting Elliott in. Now he had to do another.

THE PROPERTIES
OF SUBTRACTION

*C*harlie found Mr. Spencer in the hall at lunchtime. He was tacking up a Mathletes poster on the corkboard strip outside his classroom. It advertised the upcoming tournament and invited the rest of the student body to come watch. It was done in huge bubble letters, and he could see parts of June and Miranda and Rohan on every inch of the poster. Only Charlie was missing.

Mr. Spencer had his back to him, so Charlie coughed to get his attention. "Charlie!" Mr. Spencer exclaimed when he turned around. "We missed you on Sunday. Is everything okay?"

Charlie's stomach twisted into a tight knot. "That's what I want to talk to you about." He had thought and thought about it and tried to find some other solution. But no matter how he added it up, this was the only one that made any sense.

Mr. Spencer guided him into the classroom. "Sit down." He gestured to one of the student desks and took a seat at one himself. "What's on your mind?"

Charlie took a deep breath. Someone had written *loser* on the desk in blue colored pencil. He traced it with his finger. That was how he felt right now. "I can't be in Mathletes anymore." The words kind of jammed together coming out of his mouth, so what actually came out sounded more like "Ican'tbeinMathletesanymore."

Mr. Spencer leaned back in the chair and blew out a huge puff of air. "Man, Charlie. I'm going to be honest. I'm really disappointed to hear that."

"I know, and I'm so sorry—"

Mr. Spencer held up his hand to stop him. "Not *in* you, Charlie. Sure I'd love for you to be on the team, and I thought we could win it this year. But I'm disappointed *for* you. I thought you loved Mathletes."

Charlie's eyeballs began to prickle, and he rubbed at one of them with his hand. "I do love it. But I have to get home sooner now after school. And I can't do things on weekends anymore, so I won't be able to do competitions." What Charlie didn't say was that he wouldn't be able to watch Imogen if he was anywhere else. "It's not fair to the rest of the team."

"I respect that, but I really hope you reconsider." Mr. Spencer paused, then leaned in closer. He had a serious look on his face. "This isn't like you, Charlie. Is everything okay? Do you need to talk about anything?"

Charlie shook his head. "I'm all right." He hoped it sounded believable.

"Do you want me to call your dad, see if there's anything we can work out?"

"No, no," Charlie sputtered. That was about the worst thing that could happen. He had to keep Imogen safe and find Frank. He couldn't do that if Dad was asking questions. "You don't have to do that. I've already talked to him about this."

"All right, I understand. But know you're always welcome back."

Right now, that was only some faraway dream, but Charlie nodded. He gathered his books and lunch. Maybe he'd still have time to shove a sandwich in his face before the bell rang for the next class. On the way to the cafeteria, he passed Miranda and Rohan walking in the other direction. He tried to keep his eyes down. They passed him without saying a word.

Even though he had sealed up the passage to the other

world, it still kept subtracting things out of his life. He didn't know how to stop it.

Charlie made it home before Imogen that afternoon. Ruby was waiting for him on the porch again. Next to her was a bag from Edna's bakery. Ruby's teeth marks were imprinted in the fold.

"Did you bring these for me?" He was pretty sure Ruby nodded. She seemed especially excited to see him today and kept bumping into him with her whole body.

He opened the bag. Double chocolate chip cookies. Edna must have sent them.

He looked up when he heard a voice. "Charlie!" Elliott ran down the sidewalk, waving at him. She arrived on the front porch out of breath and collapsed onto one of the steps. "I ran all the way home and then all the way here. I'm not used to running with a heavy backpack." She caught her breath for a moment and then added, "Hey, Ruby."

Ruby licked her face in answer, and Elliott laughed.

Charlie handed her one of the cookies. "Thanks," Elliott said. "Now what's going on?"

Charlie didn't know how Elliott was going to react. Maybe she'd think he was crazy. Maybe she'd think he was making things up. But he couldn't hold it in anymore. He had to tell someone.

"I know where Frank is."

Elliott stopped mid-chew; she sprayed little cookie bits on his face. "I'm sorry, what?"

So Charlie told her the story from the beginning— starting when Imogen had told him she had seen Mom to finding the hatch and spending time with Mom in the world below. He told her about the missing memories and seeing Frank on the street and Imogen wanting to stay there forever. He showed her the pictures in the hallway with the fading Imogen and Charlie.

And at the end of the story, Charlie held his breath as Elliott said the exact thing he hoped she would. "Well, let's go get Frank back."

THE THING
ABOUT PROMISES

For the next two days after that, Charlie would burst out of the school doors when the final bell rang and race through the neighborhood, sneakers flapping. It was only when he got to the familiar red door that he would stop, put his hand out on a porch post, and take a breath.

He'd wait for Imogen on the old swing. He first saw her in the distance, running as fast as she could to the house, probably hoping to beat him there so she could go visit Mom. That was until she saw Charlie. Then she slowed to a jog and then to a walk. When she was close enough, he could see a storm cloud across her face.

He tried to talk to her but she only brushed past him.

Then she stomped through the house, threw her books around, and refused to eat anything Charlie or Dad made for dinner. He left her a note, explaining everything he was worried about, but he only found it crumpled in the trash later that night. He had thrown his Mathletes permission slip in next to it. The hardest thing was that Dad had actually remembered to sign it.

On the evening of the second day, though, things seemed to take a turn for the better. Imogen actually smiled a bit when he asked her about her school day. And she sat down with him at the kitchen table for dinner.

"There's a picnic tomorrow after school. Do you want to go?" Even though Charlie didn't plan on giving her an option, he tried to make it seem like she had one. "They'll have hot dogs and potato chips—"

"Sour cream and onion?"

They were the first words Imogen had spoken to him in two days. He had to hold on to this.

"Probably! And you'll get to see the decorations that we made, and there'll also be—"

"I'll go."

Charlie couldn't believe it was this easy to convince her. "Really? Great! You promise?"

Imogen nodded.

Charlie's shoulders relaxed, a grin spreading across his face.

Maybe this was a good time to bring up something about Not-Mom. "So there was something else I wanted to—"

"I know. You want to talk about Mom."

Yes! This was the moment Charlie had been waiting for.

"Let's talk about her tomorrow, after the picnic."

Charlie tilted his head to the side and narrowed his eyes, just slightly, to study her. Had she really turned around this quickly? Maybe, but he couldn't shake the nervous feeling that had settled in his stomach. Or maybe it was the chicken surprise Dad had left them for dinner. He couldn't quite tell.

Still, the universe kind of owed him. Maybe this turnaround was the one good thing in a line of terrible, awful things that had happened to him and his family.

He pushed aside his doubt and speared another bite of chicken. They'd talk about Mom tomorrow.

On Friday, Charlie didn't run home quite as fast. He stopped for a moment on the steps outside school to talk with Elliott. They had been working each day at lunch on a plan to save Frank. Elliott had turned it into some kind of logic problem and took notes on everything he said. They hadn't worked through everything yet, but they were making progress. Then he stopped outside Crusty's. He waved at Edna, who stood behind the counter. He thought for a moment about going in, but instead he ran on.

That is, when only three blocks from home, he heard his name.

"Charlie!"

He paused and looked around. A woman with curly hair waved at him and ran over from her car. Charlie couldn't quite see her face behind her sunglasses, but she looked a little bit familiar.

"Charlie. How are you?" she said when she reached the sidewalk. Charlie took a step back and held on a little tighter to the straps of his book bag.

"Oh gosh," the woman said, her hand flying to her chest. "I'm so sorry. You don't remember me." She removed the sunglasses. "Sandy. Sandy Dolson. I was, I mean, I'm a friend of your parents. Well, you know."

Charlie did recognize her now. She used to go jogging with Mom on Wednesdays and Fridays. "Hi." He gestured toward home. "I've got to get going so I can wait for Imogen."

He turned to leave when she caught him by the shoulder. "That's why I'm so glad I saw you. Imogen got sick at school today and went home early."

It was a full minute before Charlie's mouth and brain could form any kind of response.

"I don't understand. She went home early?"

"Well, the school called me. They couldn't get ahold of your dad, and your mom had put me on her file as a secondary emergency contact. And the nurse said that Imogen didn't feel well. So I went to school and picked her up. I offered to stay with her when I dropped her off at the house, but she told me that your dad was working from home today. I didn't see his car, but she—"

Charlie didn't even wait for her to finish her sentence before he turned and ran. He vaguely heard Mrs. Dolson calling after him, but the words got swallowed up as he put more and more ground between them. The pounding of his feet against the pavement echoed the pounding of his heart. He couldn't seem to make his feet move fast enough. It was like his legs weren't even connected to his body.

And as he ran, thoughts came at him rapid-fire.

Maybe she was really sick.

Maybe it wasn't too late.

Maybe she wouldn't go down there alone—she had promised him.

Maybe. Maybe. Maybe. Maybe.

He fumbled with his key when he reached the door. The sweat on his hands made the knob hard to grip, and he cursed as the door didn't open right away.

He kicked it and then again, letting out a cry.

Finally, a click. He pushed the door open with such force that it ricocheted back off the wall with a thud.

Imogen's backpack stood guard in the front hallway. It wasn't even unzipped. He ran through the family room.

The couch cushion where he had hidden the hammer was on the floor.

"Imogen!" Charlie yelled. "Imogen!"

There was no response.

"Imogen, please!" His voice was strained. Tears pricked his eyes, and he roughly wiped at them with his fists. He couldn't get emotional now. There wasn't time.

Imogen's door was closed. He turned the knob and pushed, but it wouldn't open.

He forced himself to take a deep breath.

He pushed again. Something was in the way. With his back against the door, he pushed again and again. Each time the door gave way a little, and he'd hear the scratch of wood against wood. Imogen's dresser. That thing was almost twice her size. How did she even—?

The thought made him push faster.

The door swung open.

"Imogen?" Charlie whispered. But the maybes had already faded.

She wasn't really sick.

It was too late.

And as his eyes swept over the bed that had been pushed aside and the hammer that lay next to her stuffed dog, and the nails, half-bent and strewn all over the room, he knew.

Imogen had gone down there alone.

AN UNEXPECTED VISITOR

*T*here was no time to wait to enact some carefully formulated plan now. Imogen was down there in the other world. Maybe she wasn't far ahead of him.

Charlie dumped out his school backpack on the floor. He might need supplies, though he wasn't sure what. He grabbed Imogen's flashlight and a jacket out of the laundry basket and two granola bars from the pantry. He stuffed them in the bag. Then he climbed down into the hatch like he had before—his arms on either side of the hole—and tried to lower himself in. But instead of the zoom-y rush and trip to the other world, nothing happened. Nothing.

He tried again, this time lowering himself down with

more force as if he could somehow rocket through to the other side through sheer will alone. But all he felt was the light bounce as the hatch rejected him.

Maybe magic words would help. He tried a bunch—*abracadabra* and *open sesame* and *open up you stupid hatch*—but none of them worked.

Charlie forced his shaking arms and legs to be calm. He had to think.

He couldn't call the police—they'd never believe him. They hadn't listened to him when they asked him about Frank months ago. Besides, he wasn't sure he would have believed it himself if he wasn't living it.

He'd call Dad. That was it. He'd call him and Dad would have to listen and then he'd come home and help. Charlie jumped up out of the hatch and ran to the kitchen. He picked up the phone and dialed Dad's cell.

The phone rang once. Twice. Three times. He heard a click.

"You've reached the voice mailbox of Charles Price, certified public accountant."

No. Charlie hung up and tried again.

He tried four times and got the same message each time. "Pick up!" Charlie yelled into the phone.

"I'm unavailable right now. Please leave a message after the beep." Unavailable right now. Unavailable forever.

"Dad," Charlie said, leaving a message. His voice cracked. "Dad, Imogen's missing. I—I—I'm going to go find her." He placed the phone back in its cradle and raked his hands through his hair and screamed. It was the sound that a caged animal makes when it realizes there is no way out.

He collapsed at the table. All the thoughts in his head jumbled together in a tangle of words and emotions. It wasn't supposed to happen like this. He didn't know what to do.

He had to get down there. But how? The only entrance was blocked. Slowly, through his thought-filled haze, he became aware of a pounding. He looked up. It was coming from the front door.

He raced through the kitchen and the front hallway, skidding to a stop in front of the door. Now, the pounding was accompanied by someone yelling his name.

"Charlie!" Pound. Pound. *"Charlie!"*

He yanked open the door. It was Elliott, hand raised mid-knock, her eyes startled. Charlie couldn't blame her—he was certain he was red-faced and disheveled and his eyes couldn't seem to focus on one thing at a time. Elliott wore her cross-country jacket and pants from her earlier practice, her hair pulled up in a high ponytail. A small star glinted right above her ear, a remnant of the decorations they were supposed to put up together.

Her words tumbled out, tripping over one another. "I

was worried about you when you didn't show up to help hang our decorations. And with everything that you told me about Frank and stuff, I thought I should come see if you were okay."

Charlie couldn't move. He couldn't speak.

In a smaller voice, she added, "Are you okay?"

And with those words, all the ones that Charlie had been holding back for months and months bubbled to the surface. He squeezed his eyes shut, willing the burning sensation away and the tears back, and shook his head. He wasn't okay.

He wasn't okay.

He hadn't been okay for a long time.

With all the words that surfaced, he chose only two. "Imogen's missing."

A SIGN

*C*harlie showed Elliott the hatch. It was one thing to talk about it and another thing to see it. She marveled at it, running her hands along the sides, opening and closing the little hatch door, scanning every crevice with Imogen's flashlight. She approached it like she might a frog under glass—something to study. Charlie showed her how to position herself in it with her arms on the side and how he'd hold his breath the moment before letting go.

Elliott tried to lower herself down into the hatch. They both hoped that maybe she'd be let through. But she experienced the same spring back that he had. This hatch didn't want her either.

"Magic," she whispered. Charlie agreed. He had once thought that magic died when Mom did. Maybe the good kind. But this magic he was dealing with now? The kind that stole Imogen? It didn't die.

It woke up.

They sat on the porch in silence, Charlie and Elliott together, just staring out at everything and nothing at the same time.

Charlie didn't know what to do. And maybe even worse, Elliott didn't know what to do. No matter how they tried to treat this like some logic puzzle to solve, there didn't seem to be any answers.

He closed his eyes and a memory popped into his head. It was as vivid and as clear as if it had happened yesterday. Mom had been lying on the couch, covered up to her neck with a blanket, and her forehead was warm and feverish. She was going in and out of sleep, but when she was awake, Charlie would feed her ice chips on a spoon.

"I need you to listen to me, Charlie," she said. Her voice was soft. He had to lean in closer to hear her, her breath hot against his ear. She grabbed his hand and held it in hers. "I'm leaving soon—"

"No," Charlie said, even though he knew it was true. Tears trailed down his face.

Mom nodded. He could tell the movement was painful

from the grimace on her face. "But I'll always be here for you and Dad and Imogen. You'll see signs of me everywhere. Little reminders when you need them."

Charlie hadn't understood what she meant at the time, and she had fallen right back asleep after that. He didn't get the chance to ask her. But he needed her right now. He needed her to be there for him and so he whispered, underneath his breath so that not even Elliott could hear, "Mom, send me a sign. Please, Mom." His voice grew more desperate. "Please."

The next thing he knew, Elliott was shaking his arm. "Look, Charlie."

He opened his eyes.

Ruby raced toward them. The tags on her bright-red collar jingled, and her nails clicked on the sidewalk, and her tongue lolled out the side of her mouth. The white spots on her fur seemed even brighter, if that was possible. Charlie thought she was going to run him over as she bounded up the porch steps, and he braced himself. Instead, she grabbed hold of his pants leg with her teeth and pulled Charlie to his feet. Then she turned and raced back in the direction that she'd come.

Charlie and Elliott stared at each other, jaws open, eyes wide. Ruby turned back to them and barked impatiently. Once, and then again.

"I think she wants us to follow her," Charlie said. And at this point, it was the only thing they had to go on.

"Let's go then," Elliott said.

As their sneakers slapped against the road, Charlie hoped that this was the sign he had asked for.

HAROLD AND EDNA

Ruby led them past the Leaning Tower of Pizza, past the little hardware store on the corner, and through Skyline's concrete patio, where they had just eaten lunch on Saturday. She always remained close enough that they could follow her but far enough that she was just out of grasp.

She skidded to a halt in front of Edna's shop and slipped inside the open door.

Charlie and Elliott followed. They stopped right at the counter, hands on their knees, trying to catch their breath.

"I've been waiting for you," Edna said, and she ushered them to the table in the back where Frank and Charlie used to sit to do homework.

"You have?" Elliott asked, confused. "I don't understand."

Charlie didn't have time to waste. "Imogen's missing." Panic beat again in his chest. Maybe this wasn't a sign after all. How could Edna possibly help? Ruby placed her head on Charlie's knee to still him. "She's in the same place Frank is."

He wasn't sure what he expected her reaction to be. Surprise, maybe. Disbelief, for sure. But instead Edna nodded and said, "I was worried that might happen."

"What? You know about the other world?" Charlie looked at Elliott and then back at Edna. "I don't get it."

"It's a long story. I think it's best to start at the beginning." Edna unclasped a locket from around her neck. It was simple and gold with a constellation of tiny jewels on the front. She popped it open. "Meet Harold." In it was a black-and-white photograph of a man, maybe a little younger than Edna. He wore a bow tie and a flower in his lapel and stared at the camera like he really loved the person behind it.

"Once, Charlie, I was just like Imogen and Frank. About ten years ago, Harold had just died, and I was alone. At least I felt alone and that there was nothing keeping me tied to the earth. I didn't want to be anywhere but with him. Then, on my first Christmas without him, I found a hole with a little door over the top of it underneath my bed."

"The hatch!" Elliott said.

"I was curious," Edna continued. "There was something that drew me to it. Harold always smelled like this mixture of cedar and aftershave. That's what it smelled like."

Charlie remembered back to the first day he had found the hatch. Mom's flowery scent had been all around it.

"I went down into it and was sucked into this other world. Most everything was the same, but—"

Charlie finished the sentence for her. "But Harold was alive."

Edna smiled a sad smile. Her eyes had a faraway look. "That's what I thought at first. I loved being back with him. We'd dance together again, and his arm around my waist felt just like it used to. Until it didn't." Charlie knew the feeling. "And I'd bake for him. I'd make the cakes and cookies he loved so much, but he always told me he wasn't hungry."

"Not-Mom was like that," Charlie said. "She'd make us dinner, but she wouldn't eat a single bite."

"That's because they don't feed on normal things like we do. They need memories to survive." Things were finally starting to fit into place. The pain he had felt at the back of his head and the not being able to remember other spaghetti dinners and scavenger hunts. Not-Mom wasn't only stealing memories, she was feeding on them. On his and on Imogen's. The thought made him want to throw up.

Elliott's face twisted up and puckered like she had taken

a big bite of a sour pickle. "What are they? They sound like some kind of monster."

"That's one way to look at it," Edna said. "You know when you shout out into a canyon and your voice returns to you? Maybe someone who's not listening very carefully might think it's your voice, but it's not. That's what these things are. They're Echoes."

Charlie thought that over slowly. "I thought it was Mom at first. But maybe because I wasn't paying close enough attention. I really wanted it to be her."

Edna nodded. "Yes. I wasn't listening carefully at first. I kept going again and again. I felt so good when I was there, but up here I felt—"

"Awful," Charlie said. "Like everything hurt."

"Exactly," Edna said. "But by the time I realized the Harold down there wasn't the Harold I knew, the Harold in here"—she tapped her heart—"it was almost too late. I had lost almost all my true memories of him."

"Like Frank?" Elliott asked slowly, considering Edna's words. "He's lost all his true memories of his grandma?"

Charlie thought about all the bowling outings and Korean dinners and trips to the amusement park—Frank wouldn't be able to remember any of them.

"He has. And that's the problem. Once you lose all your memories, you don't get to come back here, because it's like you've run out of money. You spend time there, thinking you're with the person you're missing. You give up some memories and you get to come back. If you don't have any left, well—" Edna's face was grim.

The first time Charlie had traveled from one side to the other, he had tried to go right back through from the Not-World to the real one and he couldn't—the hatch wouldn't let him through. It must have been because he hadn't given up a memory yet.

Something wild and desperate clawed at Charlie now. "How many more memories does Imogen have to give up?" He desperately tried to remember how long it had been since the time he first noticed a change in Frank to the day he disappeared. "Six months. Frank disappeared after six months. Does Imogen have that long, too?"

"It's not the same for everyone," Edna said. "Imogen's younger. She has fewer memories to give."

"So what are you telling me?" Charlie asked. He forced his voice to be calm and sat on his hands because he felt like tearing things down off the walls until everything was as upended as his life had become.

"If you don't find Imogen soon," Edna said, "she could disappear from this world forever. Just like Frank."

FOLLOW THE LIGHT

The room seemed to be shrinking in on Charlie, putting pressure on his lungs and heart. He struggled to breathe.

"Can you help her? You've been there. Go down there and save her now," Charlie said. His voice was desperate.

"If I could go down and save her, I would already be there," Edna said. "But I can't open up the door to that world again. It won't let me. I tried when I suspected that's where Frank disappeared to. I said combinations of different words and tried to wish different things, but nothing's worked." She paused for a moment, thinking. "Have you ever seen a lighthouse, Charlie?"

He nodded, though he wasn't sure why she was bringing up lighthouses at a time like this.

"Lighthouses warn approaching ships of danger. Of sharp rocks and land. Maybe that's what I'm like, Charlie. I can't sail the ship, but I can shine the light to show you the way. I'm telling you there's a way to save them. It's dangerous, but it's doable. And I think you'll have some help."

She gestured at Elliott and Ruby. "But Ruby's your dog," Charlie said.

"Ruby showed up a few months before Harold died, scratching at the door. She's been with me ever since. And right now, Ruby needs to be with you." Ruby hadn't left Charlie's side the entire time, her head resting on his leg.

Charlie looked to Elliott. "Are you in?" He couldn't even imagine how Elliott was feeling at this point. Probably the same as he was—overwhelmed, scared, uncertain. This wasn't like other adventures they had gone on, where the biggest consequence would be getting grounded. This was real. They could disappear along with Frank and Imogen.

Elliott reached over and squeezed Charlie's hand once. "You're my friend. And I want to help Frank and Imogen. Of course I'm in."

Charlie, Elliott, and Ruby started for the door.

"Remember, Charlie," Edna said. "Everyone has magic. Remember how navigators have been finding their way from the beginning of time."

Charlie looked back, and he and Edna locked eyes.

"They followed the light," she said.

"So, I guess our first step," Elliott said, as they neared their neighborhood, "is to figure out how to get to the other world. You weren't able to get through the hatch in your house, and neither was I. How did the hole get created in the first place?"

Their walk had now turned into a jog. Charlie's heart pounded in time with his feet: *faster, faster, faster.* They hadn't been at Edna's for long, twenty minutes at most, but he was certain that Imogen had lost even more memories during that time.

Charlie thought back to that night when Imogen had first found the hatch. "We were making spaghetti. I got mad. I threw the ginger at the wall."

"Ginger?" Elliott asked.

Charlie grunted and kept going. "Imogen was sad, and then she said that she wished she could go live with Mom." He stopped so quickly that he nearly tripped over his own sneakers. "That she didn't want to live with me and Dad anymore. And when she said that, the ground shook."

"It shook? Like an earthquake?"

"A little one." The pieces were clicking into place. "Her words made the hatch, didn't they?"

"We have to do it again, then," Elliott said. "Let's go to my house. Mom should be busy in her office. I can try saying words, and if that's true, a new hatch will open up under my bed. It'll be a way in."

"How do we know it will even work? I tried saying stuff and nothing happened."

"Not just random words. The right words." She paused. "And the right person. It's part of the puzzle. Think about it. Imogen's birthday. Edna's first Christmas without Harold. And—"

Elliott didn't need to say it. The end of September was when Jack died.

"Maybe those days make the missing stronger." She shrugged, her eyes focused on the sidewalk beneath her.

"But it could create a Jack. A Not-Jack."

"I know," Elliott said, her voice soft. "You have to remind me that he's not real. I don't know how I'm going to feel if I see him again. But I don't think there's any other way."

When they reached her front door, Elliott pulled her key out of her pocket and quietly slipped it into the lock. She nudged open the door, and they tiptoed in. First Elliott, then Charlie, and finally Ruby. Elliott closed the door behind them with a click and motioned them toward the steps.

"Elliott, is that you?" came a muffled voice from the basement. "You're home early from the picnic."

Charlie held his breath. Elliott turned to him with a panicked look. "Yeah, it's me. It started to rain—"

Charlie frantically gestured to the window. It was cloudy outside and getting dark, but there was no rain in sight. "Well, not rain," she continued. "More like it's just over. It didn't last too long. I thought I'd hang out here." Charlie nodded. That sounded more like something her mom would want to hear.

"I'm tired. I think I'm going to go up and read." At this point, Charlie and Ruby had already started to creep up the stairs toward Elliott's bedroom.

"All right," her mom said. "I'm going to finish some paperwork down here."

Elliott's shoulders relaxed, and she smiled a little at Charlie.

When they got to her room, Elliott shoved her desk chair against the door so that the top was wedged underneath the knob. She busied herself wrapping the cords of the hood of her jacket around one finger and then the next. "So what do I do now?" She sounded uncertain. "I feel like we're in some horror movie. Jack's not going to look scary, right?"

"He'll look normal. Better even than you remember. He's not going to look undead or anything. Remember," Charlie said, "it's not really him."

Elliott let out a deep breath she was holding. "Okay, not like a zombie."

"Not like a zombie."

Ruby nudged Elliott's hand with her nose. Elliott knelt down next to her, holding her collar. She closed her eyes. "I don't want to live here anymore with Mom and Dad." Her voice shook, and it made Charlie's insides shake. He wanted to yell for her to stop, but he couldn't seem to force the words out. They had to save Frank and Imogen. "I only want to be with Jack."

Elliott opened her eyes. They all looked at one another for a moment. It was silent. Nothing happened.

Then the shaking started, just like Charlie remembered. He tumbled across the room, his knees sinking into the soft carpet and his palms hitting her beanbag chair. Elliott crumpled all the way to the floor, taking Ruby with her.

"Elliott?" It was her mom, calling up from downstairs again. "What was that? Are you okay?"

Elliott ran to her door, pulled out the chair from underneath the knob, and opened it, yelling, "Nothing! I'm fine!" She waited until they could hear her mom's retreating steps. Then to Charlie she whispered, "Do you think it worked?"

"There's only one way to find out." Together, they braced their shoulders against the bed. It should have been harder to move than Imogen's because of the carpet underneath, but it was easier because they were working together.

As they moved the bed closer and closer to the wall, the same rough, worn wood was revealed, right where carpet had once been. "It worked!" Elliott said. She grasped the handle and pulled. If there had been a regular hole in her bedroom floor, she would have seen straight through to the garage. But now only a little bit of light peeked through.

"Ready?" Charlie said. "Actually, wait a second." A thought had occurred to him. He might not know how many memories Imogen still had, but there was a way he could track it. "Do you have a photo with Imogen in it?"

"Sure." Elliott rifled through a box of pictures on her desk. Picking one out, she gasped and held it up to the light.

Charlie sidled up next to her.

It had been Frank's tenth birthday party at the bowling alley. Charlie remembered the photograph being taken—he had been laughing because Imogen had been stuffing her face with nachos and was still mid-bite. And Frank had been goofing around with the bowling ball, making it look like he was going to drop it on Charlie's foot.

Well, there was regular-looking Elliott and Rohan and June and Grandma. And a faded Charlie and Imogen, but Frank wasn't in the picture at all. All you could see was the bowling ball suspended off the ground. Frank had disappeared from the photograph entirely.

Was this what was going to happen to Imogen, too? He shook his head to try to clear the thought and tucked the picture in his pocket. He couldn't let that happen.

He lowered himself into the hatch, and Elliott did the same. The photograph felt heavy in his pocket. He imagined that the creases and edges of the photograph were digging into his skin through the thin fabric. That was what would remind him of their mission.

Charlie grabbed Elliott's elbow and held on tight. He wouldn't let the hatch reject him this time. "On the count of three, we'll let go."

"One, two—" Elliott counted. It was now or never. "Three!"

With that, Charlie and Elliott let their arms go slack, and they dropped like they were zooming down a super-tall water slide. Ruby followed with a leap.

Then all three of them disappeared.

P/LLOW SLEDS

They landed in Elliott's room. Her other room, that is. Ruby barely clung to the left side of the hatch, her paws scrambling to find footing, so Charlie boosted her up first. Then he helped Elliott, who heaved herself over the edge.

Elliott couldn't stop picking up things around her room, looking at them like she was seeing them for the very first time. "These are my pencils," she said. "And my posters and my beanbag chair." She ran to the window. "This is my street, Charlie. My street." She lowered her voice. Her eyes went to the door. "Do you think Jack's here?"

The way she said it worried Charlie. Instead of scared, she sounded hopeful.

Ruby busied herself sniffing every crevice: underneath Elliott's blankets that covered her bed, the clean basket of laundry in the corner, and the narrow space between the door and the carpet.

"Maybe," Charlie said. He was surprised that he hadn't heard anything yet. No shouts or thundering footsteps down the stairs. Sometimes Charlie liked to imagine Jack had a windup dial on his back. He was always moving. Real Jack was loud, had a gap-toothed grin that took up his face. This version of the house, though, was quiet. Stale. "When I came down the first time, Mom was in the kitchen cooking."

"Okay." Elliott's voice trailed off, and she frowned. Maybe she expected that Jack would be waiting for them and was disappointed when he wasn't. Charlie would have to keep reminding her that if they found Jack, he wasn't the one Elliott was hoping for.

They crept out into the hallway.

"So all of this world is the same?" Elliott asked.

"I think so," Charlie said. "I think everything's the same but the people in it."

He rubbed the photograph tucked in his pocket between his thumb and forefinger. Ruby stared up at him. "We'll find them," he whispered.

"So what's the plan?" Elliott said, after she had checked all the rooms on the upstairs floor.

"I think we go to my house and try to get in. I bet Imogen's there with Mom." He didn't know where else they'd be. Each time he had come down, they had hung around inside, playing games and stuff.

"You know something that Jack and I used to do?" Elliott said. She looked wistfully at the staircase. It was a dangerous look. "When Mom or Dad weren't home, we used to take pillows from our beds and slide on our butts down the stairs. Let me show you!"

"Wait," Charlie said, but Elliott hadn't heard him as she grabbed her pillow from her room. She positioned it at the top of the steps, holding the ends of the pillowcase like a sled, and bumped down the staircase, one step at a time.

She had smiled at Charlie at the top, but by the time she got to the bottom and turned back to him, her smile had disappeared. She lifted her ponytail with one hand and grabbed the back of her neck with the other. Ruby took the steps two at a time and laid her head in Elliott's lap.

Charlie waited at the top. That was one thing he had learned in group. Sometimes you just needed to wait, to be quiet, to listen.

Elliott scratched Ruby behind the ears. She wouldn't look at Charlie. "That's not the first time I did that. I know it's not. But it feels like it is."

"I know," Charlie said. His stomach churned. He had

gotten her into this. He had done this to her. He walked down the steps and helped Elliott up. He couldn't help glancing at the picture on the front entry table. It was a picture of Jack and Elliott.

And the Elliott in this Not-World's photo was a little more solid. And the one in his pocket? A little more faded. This world was now taking pieces of Elliott. She was becoming a more permanent member of the Not-World like Frank and Imogen.

Like him.

"We have to hurry," Charlie said. And once again his heartbeat sped up. It said, *Trouble, trouble, trouble.*

THE LIST

*C*harlie went straight for the window box when they got to his house. The same two flowers stood up straight and tall. Charlie took it as a sign that Mom—Real Mom— was cheering him on.

He squatted under the window, and reaching up, he dug around till he found what he was looking for. "Bingo," he said, holding up the house key. He rubbed the dirt off on his pants.

In other circumstances, he just would have knocked on the door, knowing that Imogen and Mom were home. But he wanted to have the element of surprise on his side.

"Let's go around back." He motioned to Elliott and Ruby,

who crouched under the sight line of the windows, just in case Not-Mom was watching for them. They kept close to the house like shadows, slinking along the perimeter.

Charlie peeked in one of the back windows first, hoping that he'd see Imogen and Not-Mom sitting at the kitchen table, eating dinner. The table sat empty, but the chairs looked like they had been moved just a bit. Maybe they had finished dinner. Maybe they were somewhere else in the house.

The flutters in his chest alternated between hope and panic.

He pulled the picture out of his pocket to show Elliott. Her face was grim. She didn't have to say anything. They could both see it: Imogen was a little more faded still.

The key felt slick in Charlie's hand, and he struggled to fit it in the lock of the back door. Ruby's tail beat against his leg, like she was trying to reassure him. Finally, it slipped into place and he inched open the door. This time there were no good smells of meat loaf and spaghetti, no steam-filled kitchen or music from the radio.

Charlie, Elliott, and Ruby tried to keep their feet quiet.

They canvassed each of the rooms—the kitchen, the laundry room, the family room. All the bedrooms both upstairs and down. They even looked in the garage. Everything was quiet and still. Everything was in its proper place.

Except for Imogen and Mom. They were nowhere to be found.

The only signs that they had been there were two mugs in the kitchen sink—one ringed with chocolate along its rim and one completely clean, as if it hadn't been touched. The clean one was Mom's mug, covered with flowers on the outside. The other was Imogen's. Mom had gotten it for her special one Christmas. It had a picture of Imogen on it from her first play—it had been in kindergarten, and Imogen had been a baby bluebird. Charlie missed that smile on her face.

"So what do we do now?" Charlie asked. He held Imogen's mug in his hands like it could somehow bring her back. He hadn't expected them not to be here. They had nothing to go on now. Mom and Imogen could be anywhere.

Charlie wished he would have watched more detective shows instead of monster movies. Maybe then he'd know what to do. He knew enough about monsters, he decided. There were no monsters scarier than the one in his life.

"Okay, let's think," Elliott said. She tapped her fingers against the counter. "We have to put ourselves in Imogen's place. If I was down here and I thought I was really with my mom, I'd want to do all my favorite things with her."

That jostled loose something in Charlie's brain. About spaghetti and meat loaf and Scrabble and things Imogen had wanted to do. "The list! On our last night here together, Mom wanted to do some of our favorite things. And we left before Imogen got to do one of hers. She told Mom she had made a list."

"That's a start," Elliott said. "If everything's pretty much the same here, maybe we can find it in her room."

Charlie stumbled back down the hallway and into Imogen's room. Time was wasting, and this was the only kind-of clue they had. First, he yanked open the drawers on her nightstand—just a bunch of hair ties and charm bracelets and random art supplies she had stuffed in there. He paged through books and magazines and the script that still sat on her dresser. He even shook them out to see if anything was lodged in between the pages. Nothing. Elliott unzipped Imogen's backpack and dumped out the contents. She rifled through folders and sheets of loose leaf and her social studies notes. Ruby nosed through them for good measure. Still nothing.

Imogen had boxes of mementos in her closet. They went to those next. Light-blue boxes labeled on the outside with rectangular white stickers and precise little handwriting. Kneeling down, Charlie started in on the box that said *Photographs*. He hadn't looked through these in a long time.

Each picture was like ripping a little piece of Band-Aid off a cut. Mom and Imogen and Charlie out in the snow, looking like overstuffed marshmallows. Halloween one year when they were all different colors of M&Ms. The family picture with the giant mechanical dinosaur in Michigan. In each of these pictures, just like those in the hall, in this world both Imogen and Charlie were more solid versions of themselves. Imogen, even more than before.

And then Charlie looked at the next picture.

"Oh no," Elliott said, looking over his shoulder.

It was the same one he had in his pocket. But different. In this one, Frank and Imogen were solid, Charlie and Elliott were faded, and the other birthday party attendees were missing. A reminder of what would be if they didn't save Imogen and Frank.

He looked through the other boxes. Still no list.

He stood up and arched backward, stretching out his limbs, which seemed too tight and tense. The room was now littered with pictures and little notes and books and papers. They had found lists about Imogen's favorite Disney characters and Imogen's favorite foods and one entitled "Imogen and Lily's List of Best Actors in the School Play," and only Imogen and Lily were on the list. But there was still no list of things Imogen had wanted to do with Mom.

Then, out of the corner of his eye, he saw Ruby tugging at a piece of paper he must have overlooked. It was wedged under Imogen's stage, partially hidden by the puppet that she insisted Mom had given her only a few days ago.

Ruby pulled the paper free. Charlie took it from her and turned it over in his hands. A few of the words were smeared where Ruby's mouth had held it, and there were tooth marks in a couple of letters but he could still understand every word.

FAVORITE THINGS TO DO WITH MOM
- _Drink hot chocolate wearing our favorite slippers._
- _Go to the library and sit in the fun chairs reading books together._
- _Play at the park and eat giant pretzels with mustard._
- _Look at the night sky at the observatory._

Charlie's heart hurt looking at the list. These were all memories that Imogen was going to lose.

"Remember, there are two mugs in the sink," Elliott said. Ruby trotted over and dropped a slipper at their feet. One of Imogen's favorite flowery ones that had practically been worn through the sole. "And a slipper. So we know they've done at least one of her favorite things. If they're sticking to this list, I'd say they're probably going to the library or the park next."

"Why do you think that?" Charlie asked.

Elliott gestured toward the window. "It's not dark out yet."

She was right. Unfortunately, the park and library were in opposite directions entirely. He didn't know what to do next.

But at least they had something to go on.

MEMORIES
FOR SALE

When they stepped onto the front porch, Elliott grabbed
Charlie's shirt sleeve. "It's Jack." Her voice was fluttery,
not steady like usual.

Jack was just beyond the driveway. He bounced a big red
ball *up down, up down* and grinned at them. One of his front
teeth was still missing. Charlie gripped Imogen's list even
tighter in his fist. Ruby growled from behind his leg.

Charlie tried to be gentle with his words. He knew how
hard it was when your heart wanted to believe one thing and
your brain told you another. "It's not him, Elliott."

She scrunched her eyes closed and said, "It's not Jack, it's
not Jack. It's. Not. Jack." Then she opened one slowly. "Are

213

you sure? It really looks like him."

"Elly, what are you doing up there? Do you want to play four square?"

Elliott turned toward Charlie, her eyes now wild. "I want to play. He wants me to play."

"She can't play now," Charlie yelled. He tried to sound forceful. "We're looking for someone."

Not-Jack bounced the ball and Elliott's face got all crumply and Ruby's lips drew back in a snarl. After a moment, Jack said, "Who?"

Part of Charlie wanted to run in the other direction with Elliott and Ruby, knowing that this place was dangerous and tricky. The other part, though, whispered that maybe Jack knew something. Maybe he had seen Not-Mom and Imogen. Maybe he knew where they had gone.

The second part of Charlie won out. "Imogen—do you know where she is?"

Charlie took a step forward. Ruby dropped the slipper she was still holding, grabbed onto his shoelace, and pulled. "It's okay, girl," he said to her, but her whining only intensified and now she pushed into him, as if trying to hold him back. He shoved her gently out of the way. "It'll be fine."

"Maybe," Jack finally replied. "Maybe not."

Charlie started jogging toward Jack. Footsteps sounded behind him; he knew that Elliott and Ruby were following, only a couple of beats behind. He could hear Elliott whispering, "Not-Jack, Not-Jack," again and again under her breath.

Charlie's heart beat faster against the walls of his chest. He tugged on the bottom of his shirt and grabbed a fistful of it, wringing it in his hand, tighter and tighter. He had to stay calm. He had to ask the right questions.

"Which is it?" Charlie asked. "Either you've seen her or you haven't." His voice shook out the last few words.

"You have to give me something first."

Behind him, he heard a rustling. Then a fist thrust out in front of him, clutching a worn ten-dollar bill. "Here," Elliott said. She stepped forward and blinked rapidly. "I'll give you something. I have ten dollars." She turned to Charlie and whispered, "It's from the Pep Squad candy sale, but I'm sure they'll understand." The look on Elliott's face almost split Charlie's heart right down the middle. Here she was helping him and offering money, and this had to be the worst thing in the world for her.

"Nope," Jack said.

Elliott reached into her other pocket and pulled out three lemon drops. The wrappers were extra crinkled, the candy faded. It looked like she had been saving them for a long time. "What about some candy? You love these." She paused, catching herself. "Loved these."

"Nope."

"What do you want then?" Charlie asked, his voice more desperate now.

Jack leaned forward so close that with only one step, Elliott could have reached out and pulled him into a hug. Charlie wrapped his hand around hers and squeezed, reminding her that he was still there. Ruby nosed in between them, pressing on both of their legs.

Up this close, Charlie could see Jack's eyes. They were as empty as the street. Just like Not-Mom's. He tried to pull Elliott back, but her sneakers stayed glued to the ground below her, her eyes fixed on Jack.

Jack's grin grew. He smacked his lips together as if he were a dog waiting for a bone. "I want a memory."

UNKNOWN PROBABILITY

Charlie liked to base decisions on numbers. For example, he had calculated that there was a 75 percent chance Mrs. Lutz would collect their Spanish homework on Tuesday, and there was a 25 percent chance he and June would get in trouble for launching her potato cannon.

Numbers couldn't help him now, though. He had no idea how many memories he had lost so far, since he couldn't remember them. And how many memories did he still have left to lose?

But Jack wouldn't tell them what they needed to know without one.

Before Charlie could speak, Elliott angled herself in

front of him. "You're my brother."

"He's not," Charlie whispered, but Elliott didn't seem to hear him.

"Take one of mine," she said. She pulled her ponytail between her fingers, nervously twisting the strands.

This was something Charlie hadn't bet on.

He shook his head. "No. I can't let you do that."

"You're not letting me do anything. I am choosing this." Her voice caught. "I am choosing it. I'm going to help Imogen." Ruby whined and started to pace. Elliott put a hand on her head to still her and knelt down so they were at eye level. "I'll be all right."

Not-Jack grinned. "Tell me a story about us, Elly. A good one."

Elliott cleared her throat, grabbing Charlie's wrist and pulling him closer. He jumped as she breathed in his ear, "Please remember what I'm going to say so you can give my memory back to me later."

"Yes, I'll do that. I promise."

Elliott nodded and looked down as if she could see the memory played out on the sidewalk. "We were at this little amusement park called Coney Island and the sun, it was like an orange in the sky, so big and bright that you just thought you could reach up and take a bite out of it. And the sky was the bluest—no clouds in sight—and it honestly didn't even look real. It was like we had stepped into a fancy painting you see at the museum.

"And it was me and you"—she paused for a moment, looking at Not-Jack—"and Mom and Dad. Dad wanted some funnel cake—he only had it once a year—and the line was superlong. So Mom went and stood in line and everything smelled so delicious and fried. And you started to get antsy, so Dad said he'd take us on a ride and Mom said in her best Mom voice, 'Anything but the Ferris wheel.' You know, because we were small and Mom never liked heights. So, of course, that's what Dad took us on.

"We loaded in the cart—you were in between me and Dad, and the metal bar was snug in our laps and up we went. When we looked out at the top, you could see the Ohio River and the ferryboats and then Mom waving below, the funnel cake flying into the air when she saw us—and you just thought it was the greatest thing. You wouldn't stop laughing.

"By the time we got down to the ground, Dad was laughing and I was laughing and even Mom was laughing—kind of mad laughing but still laughing—and it was just the best day. And sometimes now, when I'm having a bad day, I think of you laughing on that Ferris wheel."

Charlie put his hand on Elliott's shoulder as his eyes started to get prickles behind them. She had never shared that with the group before. And now she'd never be able to remember it on her own again, because Not-Jack had taken it from her. But Charlie was determined to remember it for her, and he tucked it away in the cabinet of Things I'll Never Forget.

Two seconds after she had finished giving the memory, Elliott winced and closed her eyes, sucking air in through her teeth. Her hand flew to the back of her neck for the second time since they had been there, massaging the skin.

"I like that story. I want another one," Jack said.

Elliott opened her mouth, but Charlie held out his hand to stop her. It was shaking. "She's not going to tell you any more stories. Where did Imogen and Not-Mom go?"

Jack shrugged. "I don't know."

"You said you'd answer our question," Elliott said. She had her hand to her forehead now, her eyes half-closed. "Please."

Ruby growled and looked up at Charlie expectantly. Charlie shook his head. His heart began to beat faster. Elliott had given up one of her memories, Elliott was hurting, and Jack wasn't going to give them anything for it.

"I never said I'd answer any question. Try again."

Charlie grabbed the ball out of his hands and punted it across the street. "Hey," Jack said. "I was playing with that."

"You can have it back when you tell us where Imogen went."

Jack paused, like he was thinking about answering, and then said, "Nope."

With that, Charlie snapped. "Why are you so terrible?" The minute the words left his mouth, he wished he could stuff them back in.

"There's your question," Jack said. Then he laughed and laughed. But at that point, Charlie couldn't hear anything clearly because of the violent rushing in his brain. It was as if the entire ocean were between his ears.

He backed away, his eyes wide. He had wasted their question. He had wasted Elliott's memory.

He wished he could take it back. There was so much he wished he could take back.

But he couldn't. Not yet anyway. Not until he saved Imogen.

A cold nose pressed into his palm and a hand gently grabbed his elbow. Elliott said, "Let's go, Charlie."

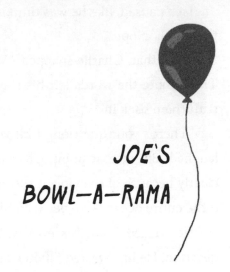

JOE'S
BOWL—A—RAMA

Charlie's cheeks burned, and he couldn't look Elliott in the eye. Ruby pushed up against his leg as if trying to keep him upright. Her touch reminded him to keep going.

He didn't know anything more about where they were headed, but he at least knew that they had to get there fast. Now Not-Mom wasn't the only Echo they'd have to deal with. They'd search the entire city if they had to. Charlie flipped up the panel on the side of the garage and punched in the code. The door opened. Bikes would be the best way to get around.

Mom's bike hung on the wall like it was waiting for her to ride it. Charlie hoped it still had air in its tires. He handed her bike to Elliott and grabbed his own.

"What about Ruby?" Elliott asked, brushing some of the dust off a helmet she found on the ground. She snapped the straps under her chin.

"There should be a wagon in here somewhere," Charlie said. He figured they couldn't quite put Ruby in their laps when they were riding or have her stand on the back wheel pegs like Frank always had when they rode together. "Maybe we can attach it to the back of one of our bikes and pull her along."

Charlie and Ruby went to the back of the garage, where the wagon normally sat tucked behind a wheelbarrow. It wasn't there. Ruby sniffed the ground around it and then dropped the slipper she had been carrying around on a little pile of dust. "What is it?" Charlie asked. He knelt down for a closer look.

There was a pattern in the dust and dirt. Tire tracks.

"I think I know where they went next!" Charlie said. "They must have taken the wagon. We'd sometimes walk to the library when it was nice out. Imogen always wanted to bring home, like, a billion books, so we'd bring the wagon."

Elliott smiled and Ruby barked. Charlie felt a little spark of joy warm his insides for a moment, the same sense of satisfaction he got when he solved a Mathletes problem. But then the spark dimmed and flickered out.

He knew how to get to Imogen. The list and the bikes—that was figured out.

What he didn't know was how to get Imogen to listen to him. To choose him, her life in the real world, and what *could be* instead of Not-Mom and what *had been*. He'd have to find a way to get through to her—and right now, he didn't have any clear solutions.

Charlie knew the way to the library, the next stop in Imogen's perfect day. A left on Markbreit and a right on Gilmore and then they were there. He remembered it being a fifteen-minute trip, but as the minutes ticked by on his wristwatch, it seemed like much longer.

Without the wagon, Ruby ran beside him, keeping pace with his front wheel, though he could hear a little whistle every time she breathed in and exhaled, like a car that was about to stall out. She had a little more gray in her fur than before. If this was hard for him, he couldn't imagine how difficult it was for her. Charlie's legs felt like the wobbly Jell-O mold that his aunt put on the table every Easter. But still, he and Elliott pedaled faster and Ruby ran harder. With every turn of the wheel, he hoped that Imogen would still be at the library.

The air was electric, like the moments right before a thunderstorm when the clouds grew dark and you just knew that any minute the sky was going to break open with rain. But the sky here was clear, no clouds in sight. It was another reminder to Charlie that this place was different. Dangerous.

They pedaled past the diner and past Edna's bakery, right up to the bowling alley, where Charlie turned his front wheel so sharply that it left a black smudge on the sidewalk. Behind him, Elliott and Ruby came to a stop, nearly colliding with each other.

"Why are we stopping?" Elliott asked. "We're still ten minutes away."

Her voice barely registered with Charlie. Instead, his eyes were trained on the bowling alley. The front door of the bowling alley that sat under the fading awning that needed to be replaced a year or so ago. The front door that Frank (or someone who really, really looked like Frank) had just disappeared into.

Charlie's brain started working the odds. He had seen Frank down here once before. He was sure of it, even though Not-Mom tried to convince him he hadn't. He had seen him walking with Grandma, but more likely Not-Grandma, as the only people who seemed to exist in this world were sad, grieving people and Echoes who pretended to be the people they missed.

They had planned to save Imogen first, and then

somehow find Frank for real this time. But if this was Frank now, Charlie couldn't leave him behind.

"Frank!" Charlie screamed. He hopped off the bike, letting it fall to the ground with a crash. He ran with Ruby right on his heels. And he determined that if he got out of this place (no, *when* he got out of this place), he'd go out for track or maybe cross-country with Elliott, because man, he had done a lot of running.

As he ran, he tried to put together a plan in his head. Okay, he'd find Frank really fast so he could go find Imogen and bring her home.

Good. He had a plan.

He swung open the door to the bowling alley, not really sure what he was going to find. Usually, there'd be half-eaten popcorn pieces dotting the ground, crunching under his sneakers. And the place would kind of smell like the aerosol foot deodorizer that they sprayed in the shoes after you wore them. And you'd hear the electronic beeps and whirs of the Pac-Man and pinball games in their two-game arcade, not counting the claw machine, where one time Charlie won a stuffed purple armadillo, mixed in with the crash of the ball hitting the pins. Or the ball rolling down the gutter, in the case of Frank's grandma.

The only thing Charlie heard, though, when he walked in was a lone ball hitting the pins, followed by a pause as the pins reset, and then the ball hitting the pins again. Using the half wall in the entryway to conceal himself, he put both hands on the edge and peered around.

Slowly. Slowly, so that only his eyes and a little bit of his face were showing if someone were to glance over.

At the far end of the bowling alley, at their lucky bowling lane, was Frank sitting in the chair in front of the scoring screen. Not-Grandma rolled the ball down the lane with what seemed like superhuman strength. In real life, she could barely even pick it up.

"A strike again, Grandma." Frank's voice sounded mechanical, as if he were a robot and not a boy who used to build tall newspaper towers using scientific principles and follow the stock market, where he had invested fake money in a math project with Mr. Spencer.

Charlie felt a whoosh of air as the front door opened again. He motioned to Elliott to crouch down next to him and Ruby. He wished that he would have come up with a better plan. Get Frank out quickly sounded good four minutes ago, but he was missing all the steps in between. Like, how to distract Not-Grandma—no matter who she was, Charlie couldn't knock over an old lady. And maybe how to convince Frank to come with them. Frank, like Imogen, might not want to leave. Would he even remember them?

He whispered to Elliott, "What are we going to do?"

Elliott stuck her head over the half wall for a second or two and then popped back down. "Okay, I'll run over to the arcade and create a distraction, like I really want to play one of the games. Or like maybe someone's stuck in the claw machine. You go grab Frank."

Ruby looked at Elliott, her head cocked to the side. The white spots on her fur looked even more like stars than before. Like constellations almost. "And Ruby, you chase Frank's grandma if needed." Elliott scratched her behind the ears.

If there was a merit badge for making plans or for bowling alley recon, Elliott would certainly get it. Charlie nodded and gave a thumbs-up.

"On my count," Elliott whispered. "One, two, THREE!"

THE ROLE OF INVERSE
OPERATIONS

*E*lliott jumped up and ran, flailing her arms. "I want to play some games. Yay, games! I call dibs on Pac-Man."

The bright red and yellow and blue flashing lights from the arcade painted a rainbow on Elliott's ponytail as it bobbed up and down. Charlie watched from his hiding spot as both Frank and Not-Grandma turned to look.

He then braced himself and popped up. Not-Grandma had taken steps toward Elliott, who was dancing around the arcade, hitting the buttons as she went. Not-Grandma turned when she heard running and seemed to freeze in time—looking one way and then the other, seemingly unsure of which direction to turn. Then she darted into the arcade.

But Charlie couldn't worry about that now. He had to worry about Frank—Frank who seemed frozen, too, like his sneakers were bolted to the floor. Charlie's shoes echoed off the squeaky wood as he walked toward Frank. He kept watching for the look in Frank's eyes to change. For them to show some little flash that he remembered Charlie and Elliott and Ruby.

His eyes remained blank.

When Charlie reached him, he took him by the shoulders and shook him a little bit. "Frank, it's me. Charlie."

Frank just stared right through him as if Charlie wasn't there.

Charlie wanted to scream. He had to think. Then something Elliott had said earlier struck him. When she gave up her memory to Not-Jack, she whispered to Charlie that he'd have to help her remember.

He'd have to make Frank remember.

"Remember how we'd go to the Leaning Tower of Pizza and you'd always eat your crust first and I said it was weird? But then I did it and it was delicious—the perfect bread-to-sauce ratio. And when we were in fourth grade, we'd play Around the World in math class and you'd always beat me at multiplication facts. Especially the twelves."

Frank's eyes grew just a bit brighter—barely noticeable. But Charlie noticed.

"You and me and Rohan—we did that thing with the Mentos and Diet Coke outside your house and it spurted all over your grandma when she came out to watch. We were worried she'd be mad, but she only laughed and helped us load up the next bottle."

Frank's eyes took on even more color now.

This was the most important Mathletes problem Charlie had ever solved. He had buzzed in.

Question: How do you save Frank?

Answer: Inverse operations. The inverse of multiplication was division. The inverse of subtraction was addition. As Charlie gave Frank memories, they seemed to counteract the ones Not-Grandma had taken away.

"Remember, we'd play this thing, Frank, where we'd ask each other questions and then say the answer and then say it was—"

Frank's eyes shifted, and he looked at Charlie like he was finally coming into focus. "For the game show," he said.

"Yes! For the game show!" Charlie said, pulling Frank in for a hug. And it wasn't even like a boy hug where you clasp your hands together and pound your chest and slap each other on the back. This was a real hug with real Frank.

His best friend.

Hugging Frank and thinking back to all the great things they had done together helped fill a bit of Charlie's emptiness.

"So I've got a question, Frank. For the game show—will you come with us?"

Frank looked around—at the lane where he had just bowled with Not-Grandma and at the beeping Pac-Man game in the arcade. Charlie held his breath. Maybe he was looking for Not-Grandma. Maybe he wanted to stay.

Finally, Frank whispered, "I'll go."

Charlie wanted to cheer as Mom had. *Hypotenuse! Pythagorean theorem! Parabola!* Charlie grabbed Frank's arm and started running for the exit when he realized that not only was Not-Grandma nowhere to be seen, but he had also lost track of Ruby and Elliott.

Charlie slowed. "Elliott," he called out. He paused another three seconds, and then said in a quieter voice, "Ruby."

No one. Charlie didn't want to let Frank out of his sight. He was worried that if he left his friend for one small second, Frank would disappear again. Poof. Charlie wasn't sure his heart could handle that.

So instead, they walked around the bowling alley together—canvassing the lanes and the arcade and the food bar.

232

Finally, a bark sounded and Ruby appeared outside the entrance to the bowling alley. Charlie opened the door. Ruby had a ponytail holder in his mouth. In Lincoln Middle School colors. The kind that Elliott liked to wear. The kind she was wearing today.

"Elliott." Charlie finally exhaled. "Someone's got Elliott." At this point, Charlie could barely hold himself up, much less Frank. The entire world was crumbling beneath his feet.

Ruby grabbed onto Charlie's pant leg and pulled him out of the bowling alley into the empty parking lot. The sun was almost hidden away behind the horizon, but Charlie still blinked as his eyes adjusted.

Charlie saw Elliott just before she disappeared around the corner. She was hand in hand with a little boy, who turned and looked at Charlie for just a second. He had a large one-toothed smile.

"Jack," Charlie said. "Her brother came back to get her."

CROSSING
THE STREET

*C*harlie wished that someone would just tell him what to do. Frank. Imogen. Elliott. The names cycled through his mind at a rapid pace—a motor he couldn't turn off.

Slow down, Charlie, slow down, he told himself. And he wiggled his fingers, then clenched them in a fist and relaxed them. He took in a deep breath and let it out. His mind slowed and the tingly feeling that had built up in his hands faded until it was barely noticeable.

He pulled the picture out of his pocket. Imogen was a little more faded.

Charlie felt that way, too. Even though Not-Mom wasn't taking his memories away at this moment, he didn't have

Imogen or Dad or Mathletes or Elliott. The Echoes were still stealing away the things he loved.

"Do you think you could take a bike?" Charlie asked. He didn't think he could handle both on his own. They'd only slow him down, and they might need them later.

Frank, still dazed and quiet, nodded. Charlie wished that he had time to ask Frank how he was and where he'd been all this time down here. He just had so many questions and so many things he wanted to say.

Like that he was sorry. Sorry for everything—for being a bad friend, for not finding him sooner, for not understanding more. Charlie was brimming with apologies.

But he couldn't say them now. There wasn't time.

"Elliott," Charlie called out, hoping that she might still be close enough to hear him. "Elliott!" They set off, pedaling in the direction in which she'd disappeared. Ruby kept her eyes and nose to the ground, sniffing out her path, leading the way.

He tried to think back to the things Elliott talked about in group. It was strange that memories now served as clues. He remembered how she told them about making fake stew with Jack in their backyard using leaves and twigs. How they'd eat Popsicles in the summer on the giant hill in their yard, looking up at the clouds. And how Elliott wasn't holding Jack's hand when the car hit him and if she had just been holding his hand—

When Ruby veered right onto Isabella Avenue, Charlie knew where they were going.

No.

No.

He couldn't stand to see Elliott in pain again. Charlie didn't want to go. There was still a little plaque there with Jack's face and a ribbon on one of the tall electricity poles— Charlie passed it on the days when he'd take the back way home from school. And when he did, he'd try to remember to walk on the other side of the pole so he wouldn't see the plaque straight on, because remembering was hard.

Familiar shops and trees and roads blurred together into something that a three-year-old might create for a spot on the refrigerator. Charlie's moves became automatic. A turn here, sailing over the curb there. His legs became automatic, too. Then he saw Elliott in the distance. Ruby barked, but Elliott didn't look up. She was crouched down, her hand on Jack's shoulder—Jack, with his floppy brown hair and scraped knees. Jack, who couldn't stop laughing on the Ferris wheel. Charlie watched her stand and then take Jack's hand.

Time slowed and Charlie couldn't move fast enough. He couldn't move fast enough. He was off his bike and could see his arms outstretched in front of him, and he was pretty sure he was saying something because his mouth was moving, but he wasn't sure what.

But Elliott and Jack looked up, and it bought Charlie a second. Or two.

Elliott grinned and waved. Jack just stood there, his eyes narrowed at Charlie, his mouth drawn into a thin line almost like a cartoon character. This wasn't the Jack from the Ferris wheel.

"What are you doing?" Elliott said, as Charlie reached her. She looked confused and took a step back. Charlie bent over, hands on his knees, trying to force his breath back inside his lungs. "Look who found me again." She grinned. He could see parts of Jack in her smile, in her freckles. "Jack's sorry about before, Charlie. He didn't mean it. We're going to go to the zoo, like I promised him. Only it's very important that we cross the street together, making sure that we look both ways for cars. That's right, isn't it, Jack? That's what Mom taught us."

Jack smiled, but not a Real Jack smile—not a smile like in the pictures Elliott had on her desk.

Frank stepped next to Charlie. He didn't say anything, but him just being there made Charlie feel stronger. "This isn't Jack."

Something flashed across Elliott's face, but then it was gone. "We were wrong, Charlie. Jack's not like the others. It's really him, and he wants me to stay." The hand that wasn't holding Jack's reached out to Charlie. Her fingers circled his arm, and all he could think about was how her fingernails looked like brightly colored jelly beans and they were on his arm. Then he looked up. Her eyes were pleading—trying to make Charlie understand. "He missed me."

This was bad. Pain thrummed through Charlie's insides—ten times worse than one of his headaches had ever been. It was one thing to have all this happen to you. But it was another entirely to have it happen to Elliott. To watch her hope be taken away.

"And he tells me that if I cross the street with him, I'll forget all the other times I crossed the street with him. And I need that to happen." Her eyes went to the plaque on the pole and then to the sidewalk. "I want that to happen." Her voice grew desperate. "I need to forget because this moment plays in my head again and again and I can't turn it off."

The light above them turned from green to red and the walk sign illuminated.

He had to keep Elliott talking. "How many times did you cross the street with Jack, or hold his hand?"

Jack was now yanking on Elliott's arm. Ruby growled and jumped at him, but Jack only pushed her back. "Bad dog," he snarled. Then he turned to Elliott, his voice sweet again. "The walk sign is up, Elly. Let's go! I want to see the rhinos."

But still, Elliott remained. "I don't know. Hundreds. Thousands maybe."

"And you're willing to give all of those up for this? For one walk across the street?" Charlie didn't tell her that he had sometimes lain in bed after he had come back from the other world, thinking about what bad memories he could relive and then give up. Bad memories that seemed to crowd out the good ones and play over and over again in his head, like a song Imogen had set on repeat.

But Elliott and her memories were worth saving. "This isn't Jack, Elliott."

Elliott's face drooped like melting ice cream in the sun, losing its shape.

She whispered. Her hand was still on Charlie's arm, and he concentrated on the heat on his skin. He stepped closer.

She whispered again. "It was my fault."

"It was my fault," Charlie whispered. Brightly colored pills were strewn over the tile—ovals and circles. He sank to his knees and began scooping them up in one hand. "I'm so sorry." But his words were muffled and his shoulders shook.

He half glanced up at Mom, who still sat at the breakfast table. She wasn't looking at him or even at the pills on the floor. Instead she stared at the turned-over brown and white bottles on the table. The ones Charlie had just turned over.

Mom had asked him to help open one—she had

seven—and he couldn't get it. The cap was stuck. Childproof?
Try Charlie proof. He couldn't do the one thing that would
help her. And without thinking, he threw the bottle at the
table, knocking over the others, spilling them onto the floor.

He wanted her to scream at him, to yell, to ground him,
to get angry. But she only shook her head and bent over, grab-
bing his hand. She cupped it in her own.

"It's okay, Charlie. It's okay." And he buried his head
in her knee while he cried. She made shushing sounds and
stroked his hair.

Later, he'd replay the moment in his head again and
again, wishing he had done things differently. Wishing that
he wasn't so angry. Wishing that he had been the one there
for Mom, instead of the other way around.

He could be here for Elliott now.

"It wasn't your fault." He could see Jack's grip tighten on
her hand. She swayed as Jack once again tried to pull her
into the street. "Sometimes things happen and sometimes
they're terrible and unfair. But they don't erase the awesome
stuff. They don't erase the stuff we love. Life's not some scientific balance."

He didn't even know where these words were coming
from. Grief group, maybe. Elliott couldn't leave behind all
the great things that had built her up and made her Elliott.
Or the sad things. Dr. Miller had asked them to close their

eyes and picture it one time—all the moments that had happened in their lives. Those moments were like their DNA,
weaving together the fabric of who they were. They couldn't
just cut away the bad stuff and only take the good or else
the fabric would be full of holes. *That's life,* she had said.
*And you are not Swiss cheese. So when the good comes along,
you've got to hold on to it.*

He needed Elliott to hold on to the good.

"Jack loved you, Elliott," Charlie said, his voice softer.
"He needed you, and you were there. That's who you are.
When something happens, you show up."

Elliott looked from Not-Jack to Charlie and then back
again. Charlie could see Jack's grip on her slip a little.

"We need you to be here with us now."

Frank spoke up now, surprising Charlie. "Stay with us,
Elliott."

"The light's going to turn soon," Jack said. Charlie could
hear the gritted teeth in Jack's voice. "Who are you going to
choose, Elly? I can make all your bad memories go away. You
can stay here with me."

Elliott closed her eyes.

A moment passed. The countdown light flashed from
four to three to two.

Charlie grabbed Elliott's hand and held it tightly in
his own. Sometimes that was the only thing you could do.

There was no merit badge to earn or club to join for facing these things head-on. But he had seen her courage when she hadn't hesitated to come here with him.

Then she said, "I choose Jack. The real one. And I choose everything that comes with it."

And with those words Not-Jack began to flicker. His shape morphed—taller, then shorter, bigger, then smaller until it was something that neither of them recognized anymore.

Then he disappeared into the twilight.

SOMETHING WORTH
FORGETTING

On vacations the two things Charlie's family always found first were the local bakery and the library. "Different kinds of treats," Mom would say. On the beach, at a lighthouse, waiting in line at Disney, no matter where it was, she'd have a pastry in one hand and a book in the other.

At their own library, Charlie would go straight to the nonfiction section; Imogen to the play area, where they had a storytelling stage, and then to the books about Pippi Longstocking and her favorite series, the Doll People. And Mom loved anything—mysteries, sci-fi, fantasy—but she had one requirement: the characters had to be brave.

Later, when Mom was in the no-hair, tissue-paper-skin

stage and he could trace the blue and red veins in her skin like a road map, Charlie asked her about it. He was asking her about everything then, rushing to fit in all his unanswered questions.

That was the tricky thing about dying, he determined.

It felt slow and fast all at once.

Mom told him that brave characters reminded her of Imogen and Charlie.

Walking up the steps to the library, Charlie felt whatever the inverse of brave was.

They had been quiet the whole rest of the way over. Elliott insisted that Frank and Charlie take the bikes—she was the fastest and ran alongside with Ruby.

He wanted to find out more about this world from Frank. He wanted to talk about what Frank had been through and what had just happened with Jack. But Frank, who had once worn that hot dog shirt and danced into class and would break out into songs he had made up on the spot, seemed to shrink under their stares. When a meteor enters the atmosphere, the force of entry and gravity wear away at the rock until there's maybe only a pebble left when it finally hits the surface. Charlie hoped that entering back into their atmosphere wouldn't do the same to Frank.

Charlie nodded at him. Frank seemed to take it as encouragement.

"I don't know if I'm going to be able to go back with you," Frank said suddenly. Immediately, his shoulders lifted a bit, like he was now somehow lighter for saying it.

"What do you mean—" Charlie began, but then Elliott kicked him lightly in the shin. Charlie couldn't believe, though, what Frank was saying.

"I want to go back. I really want to go back," Frank said. Then he paused, and his eyes began to grow watery. He scuffed the step with his sneaker. Charlie noticed that his feet seemed to be crammed into them. Frank had grown down here and his shoes hadn't.

"Well, we'll go back," Charlie said. He reminded himself that Frank had been stuck here, away from everyone. He needed to be patient. "We're together now."

"But the thing is," Frank said. His voice quivered. "I've tried to go back. A lot of times, and the hatch wouldn't let me, Charlie. I don't know why it would be any different this time."

Elliott took Frank by both shoulders and looked him straight in the face. "There has to be a way. We're not leaving you behind. We're not leaving anyone behind." Ruby barked her agreement.

Frank sniffled and rubbed his eyes with the sleeve of his T-shirt.

"Okay," he said.

When Frank turned back toward the entrance, Charlie frowned and caught Elliott's eye. He could tell she was thinking the same thing. They knew that Frank hadn't been able to come back. But for whatever reason, Charlie had thought that their just showing up would make the difference. Now he wasn't so sure. Frank didn't have any memories left to give.

They'd have to think of something. Elliott was right: no one was getting left behind.

Charlie opened the door to the library. Normally the glass-paneled front revealed kids tucked away in corners with stacks of books piled as tall as them, but not this time. There wasn't even a librarian at the front information desk.

Charlie wished that he had some kind of weapon with him now—a baseball bat, a hockey stick, gosh, he'd even take some kind of broom.

"I think we should split up," Elliott said, turning to face the group. "This is a big library. We'll cover more ground this way. Imogen still could be here." She lifted up on her tiptoes, just a bit. Her words hung in the air—hopeful and desperate at the same time.

The library was big—three huge floors, two outdoor walled gardens. It was essentially two buildings connected by a bridge in the middle. He had to pick a place for them to begin looking. "Frank, why don't you and Ruby check out the fiction section," Charlie said. At least they could look in pairs—that would be safer than going alone. Frank nodded. Ruby stood right beside him, so that her body was touching his leg. Charlie knew that Ruby would look out for Frank.

"Elliott and I will go check the kids' section with the stage. Those are the most likely places we'll find her. We'll meet at the front entrance in"—he glanced at his watch—"fifteen minutes. But yell if you see or hear anything."

Frank and Ruby turned down a hallway on the left while Charlie and Elliott started for the stairs, taking them two at a time. When they reached the top, Elliott grabbed his hand and whirled him around. She had been quiet on the entire bike ride over. So had Charlie—he had thought of about nine thousand different things to say to her, like *Are you okay?*, but couldn't seem to push the words out.

Her mouth opened once, and then closed. Then it opened again. It reminded Charlie of the goldfish behind glass at Elmer's Pet Shop. Finally (though it was probably just a few seconds), words came out. "Charlie, I'm really sorry for what happened back there with Jack and I know that it slowed us down and I feel so awful about it. Like so, so awful. And this is all my fault just like Jack and—"

Charlie put his hand on her wrist. He could feel her heartbeat through his fingertips. He had never felt a hummingbird's heartbeat, but he imagined that this was what it would feel like. He took a deep breath.

"I'm sorry, too. For before. For the memory. And getting angry and wasting our question." He paused. "Jack wasn't your fault. And Imogen is not your fault. We're going to save her." They had to. Charlie just had to channel the brave kid Mom thought he was.

Elliott nodded once. Twice. He imagined her pushing all the feelings down to her shoes like he did. But maybe there were fewer bad feelings to push down than before. She stood up a little straighter. "Okay." And the corners of her mouth turned up the smallest bit.

They crept along the side of one of the stacks. Charlie motioned Elliott to look ahead while he peered through the gap between the top of the books and the shelf above it. They zigzagged between the rows, taking one at a time.

Finally, a pull on his shirt. The signal.

Elliott's eyes were wide. She pointed at a pair of chairs, both in fun shapes like the ones on Imogen's list. They sat across from the storytelling stage, which was now littered with princess costumes and wands with stars on the top and puppets. In between the chairs was a stack of books. Charlie paged through them—he had seen them before on Imogen's nightstand. They were some of her favorites. Then he felt the seat of one of the chairs with his palm—it was still warm.

Now Charlie wished they had stayed together. Maybe

Ruby would have been able to tell them which direction to go next. "They have to be around here somewhere!" he whispered. He didn't know whether he should shout Imogen's name or try to sneak up behind her. He grabbed Elliott's hand and they ran to the next section of books. Charlie kept waiting for some librarian to yell at them to stop running, but all he could hear were their footsteps.

At once, Charlie spotted a pouf of blond hair disappearing behind one of the walls ahead. He gave up on trying to be quiet. "Imogen!" he shouted. "Imogen! She just went into the film section." He hoped that wherever Frank and Ruby were, they could hear him. Maybe they could cut her off somewhere or block the exits.

He darted down one of the aisles. Out of the corner of his eye he saw a flash of red and then a streak of blond. They were an aisle away. Charlie's legs pumped and his arms pumped and he couldn't breathe, but he kept going and at the end of the aisle he leaped. His fingertips caught onto the back of Imogen's sweatshirt.

He had her! He had her!

Not-Mom held on to Imogen's hand, pulling her ahead. Imogen turned back. Their eyes met. Charlie's mouth formed the word *please*, but no sound came out. Imogen grabbed her sweatshirt with her free hand, and she twisted it out of his grasp. Without something to hold on to, Charlie tumbled forward. His knees hit the ground first, and his worn jeans ripped. His palms hit next. Pain shot up through his arms all the way to his shoulders. Still, right before he face-planted, he managed to yell to Elliott to keep going.

And as he lay on the ground for the two seconds before action became reaction, he concentrated on the pain shooting through his body. But what hurt even worse was the look Imogen had given him when she turned around—her eyes narrowed, her face twisted, cheeks flaming. The look burned into his brain, becoming part of his memories.

That moment—along with all of the moments he had failed Mom—was another thing he wouldn't mind forgetting.

THE ESCAPE

It didn't seem like long at all between the time that Charlie was splayed out on the floor and then upright in the front lobby, but it was enough time for Not-Mom and Imogen to slip away.

Elliott stood just inside the door to the library, her hand cupped over her eyes, staring out into the fading sunlight, like if she looked hard enough, they'd suddenly reappear. Ruby's fur stood on end, near her hind legs. She growled and sniffed around the entrance, trying to trace their path.

Charlie kept replaying the moment in his mind. The bit of sweatshirt in his hand. The look on Imogen's face. She had chosen, and she hadn't chosen him. His knees stung from his fall, but her decision hurt the most.

Frank inched closer to Charlie and put his hand on his shoulder. "Don't give up," he said. "It took me a long time to see all that I was missing." Frank's words almost broke Charlie right in half. He had missed his friend so much, and here he was sounding much more like Frank than he had in a long time.

But Imogen was still gone. And they were still in this Not-Place. Still in danger. He pulled out the photograph from his pocket and traced Imogen's outline. He could barely see it now. But Frank, who had once been missing from the photograph, was slowly coming back into view. Maybe this had happened in the bowling alley, when Charlie had given him back a memory.

Ruby walked up next to Charlie, her fur tickling the bottom of his fingertips. "Frank's right," Elliott said. "We just have to find Imogen and make her understand." She waited till Charlie looked at her. "We're not leaving anyone behind, remember?"

"So what's the plan?" Frank asked.

"She wanted to go to the park to play and get a pretzel, right?" Elliott said.

Charlie nodded. "There are three possible places she could get a pretzel." He was thankful, at that moment, for what Rohan called the Summer of Pretzels, where they had tasted all the pretzels Cincinnati had to offer and ranked them according to Rohan's carefully calibrated scale. Charlie hadn't been able to even *look* at a pretzel after that for months, but it did give him a close knowledge of where everything was located. "On Madison, on Paxton, and on Logan."

"They'll probably go to the one on Paxton. It's the closest to the observatory," Elliott said. "If they're not at the concession stand, we can cut through the park and maybe beat them there." She clapped her hands. "Let's go!"

The sky wasn't all the way dark but in the glow-y in-between stage that he and Imogen loved because it meant that they got to stay outside a little bit longer. But today, Charlie wanted it to get dark outside as soon as possible. He couldn't see all the stars in the sky this way. He couldn't watch for them to blink out like he had on the last night with Mom. He couldn't tell when Imogen had lost another memory.

The brick sign at the entrance of the park had two tiny spotlights on it, illuminating the lettering. Behind that, the sun had just dipped below the hill.

"The concession stand is this way," Charlie said. The paved trail wove in between hills, and they passed the jungle gym on the left. One of the swings rocked back and forth as if someone had just jumped off it into the air. Maybe Imogen.

They pulled in front of the tiny brick enclosure that housed the Snack Shack. It had received a rating of 4.7 out of 5 on Rohan's pretzel scale. Charlie rode up to the glass windows in the front and tried to push them open. They didn't budge. Cupping his hands around his eyes, he pressed his face against the glass.

No oil bubbled in the fryer, and the popcorn machine only had a few unpopped kernels, though the red-and-yellow light on top glowed. And the metal hooks, where the pretzels hung when they were hot and ready, were empty.

There were no telltale bits of salt on the counter or traces of that orange processed cheese topping that Imogen loved so much.

Charlie's stomach would have only hurt more, he thought, if he had gotten socked in the gut. His toes curled. "I think we're at the wrong one," he said.

But when he turned back, no one was looking at him. Instead, they were looking at a little plaque nailed to a wooden pole, surrounded by tiny white flowers. To the right of that was a wooden bench. Charlie had walked by it a million times, never taking a closer look.

"It's Edna," Elliott said.

Charlie read the plaque aloud. "'In memory of Harold Morrison. Friend to the park system and amateur astronomer. He and his wife, Edna, cataloged over three thousand stars before his death.'" There was a picture etched into it of Edna and Harold together on the tallest hill of the park, looking up to the sky, a telescope perched on a tripod about waist high.

And at their feet there was a dog. Charlie leaned into the picture, his nose almost touching it. He then looked back at Ruby. Then back at the picture. "Is this you?" he asked Ruby. Ruby wagged her tail in response.

There were some little differences. Ruby had thicker eyebrows, for one, and the dog in the picture had a different-shaped nose. But the patterns on the dogs' fur and the look in their eyes were exactly the same.

Charlie wasn't sure what this all meant. But what he did know was that it had gotten darker, and as he turned to the sky, another star disappeared. Just like it had when he had been looking through the telescope with Imogen and Not-Mom. The sky down here wasn't like the sky in the other world, where the number of stars seemed infinite. Here, you could count the stars one by one.

There weren't many left now.

"On to the observatory?" Charlie asked. Seeing Edna on the plaque and the dog that looked like Ruby, knowing that Frank and Elliott were down here with him, he suddenly knew that this wasn't just about him, or about Imogen. This was about something much, much bigger and older.

Something that had been happening since the beginning of time.

Edna was right. She was a lighthouse keeper, shining the path he needed to take through the dangerous waters of the Not-World. And Charlie was the captain. He knew what he needed to do. He needed to steer the ship.

"Let's go," he said, and they rode into the night.

THE OBSERVATORY

As they rode closer, he could see that the observatory looked like a star itself—lit up, its white dome standing out against the night sky. But this time, instead of his usual buzzy excitement, the image made Charlie swallow hard. They slowed to a stop in front of it. Charlie hopped off his bike first, leaning it against the brick-and-concrete staircase. Imogen's red wagon was already there.

He should have raced up the steps. But he knew what he had to face inside.

He had done the same thing at Mom's visitation. He had waited, right outside the door at the funeral home, until his aunt Emily had pushed him in. He had just wanted one minute of not having to face it.

But a minute now could mean losing Imogen forever.

No one had to push him this time.

Grasping the handle of one of the large white doors, which were at least twice as tall as he was, he pulled. It wasn't locked, and creaked open. The sound startled him because until now, the only sound had been that of their breathing and the *clink clink* of their bicycle wheels.

He looked back for just a moment. Frank, Elliott, and Ruby stood behind him, shoulder to shoulder (and in Ruby's case, shoulder to knee). Force multiplied. Gravity pulling them together. Ruby pressed her nose into his skin, right where his jeans had ripped on the knee.

How could he have ever felt alone?

Frank nodded, and that one small motion helped Charlie pull open the door the rest of the way. They crowded into the entrance, and the door shut behind them, closing out the last little sliver of light from the streetlamps and leaving it on the outside.

Charlie shrugged off his backpack. He found the zipper and opened it. He fumbled around in the backpack for a moment or two, until his fingers latched onto what he was looking for. Grabbing the flashlight, he clicked it on.

Sometimes you had to make your own light.

He swept the beam across the room, all the while holding his breath. The darkness pressed in on him, squeezing his insides, so instead, he focused on everything the beam illuminated. The front welcome desk, which sat empty. The fancy rug and shelves of books that made up the tiny library—full of information about the stars and planets. And the old wooden staircase that led up to his favorite telescope—the one people first used in 1904.

After Imogen had visited the observatory, she had written stories about who those people were and made up conversations they had as they saw the night sky up close for the very first time.

There had to be a next time for her.

By now, Charlie had memorized Imogen's list, so there was no need for him to look. He knew she'd be with Not-Mom, looking up at the sky through the very telescope he loved. There weren't many stars left to see.

Their eyes had now adjusted to the dark, and they could at least see the outlines of the objects that surrounded them. Charlie motioned with his hand to the wooden staircase. As they crept closer, he willed their feet to be quiet. His heart was in his ears, but in between the rapid *thump thump thumps* was Imogen's voice.

"Tell me a story." His heart contracted at the sound. A teacher had once described Imogen's voice as musical. It didn't sound like that now. It wasn't as robotic as Frank's had been, but close.

Charlie knew the story Not-Mom would tell—the story

of the dragon. His sneaker hit the first step.

"It's just a small story," Not-Mom began. Charlie's face grew hot. This wasn't her story to tell. He clicked off the flashlight, tightened his grip. The light that came through the opening in the top of the dome was enough for him to see. He skipped the next step entirely. She continued, "Once, a long time ago, there was a god named Zeus."

As she spoke, Charlie changed the narration in his mind. *Once upon a time, there was a boy named Charlie. Who loved his sister. Who wasn't like the boy in the story of the dragon.*

Charlie stood, both feet planted on the final step. His eyes were fixed on Imogen and Not-Mom. Not-Mom's hand on Imogen's shoulder, Imogen's face pressed up against the eyepiece of the telescope. Both of them turned away from Charlie. His gaze didn't waver.

"But the brother never found his sister," Not-Mom said.

"No," Charlie said, and then a little louder, "At the end of this story, he'll save her."

REWRITING THE ENDING

*N*ot-Mom looked up as Charlie stepped into the telescope room. Her hand never left Imogen's shoulder. "I'm glad you could join us for a story or two, Charlie. I was just telling Imogen one of your favorites."

"You don't know anything about me," Charlie said. In his head, his voice sounded courageous, but out loud it only sounded unsure. He shoved his free hand in his jeans pocket.

"We're all together now," Imogen said. She sounded as if she was speaking through closed teeth. She pulled away from the telescope. The telescope was beautiful and big. It was an organized mess of gears and tubes and dials in white and gold. They had aimed it at the top of the dome, where

261

the ceiling split, leaving only a slice of sky.

Only a handful of stars remained.

"I told you he'd come. I knew he'd understand." Imogen reached out to Charlie, but Not-Mom held her back. Charlie made a tight fist. If he was going to save Imogen, he couldn't blow up.

"Ruby's here. Frank, too."

"Frank, really?" Imogen craned her neck to see.

Unlike some other guys from his class, who hated when little sisters hung around, Frank had always listened to Imogen in a way that showed you he really meant it. He liked playing her imagination games. They were a lot alike, actually.

Frank, Elliott, and Ruby entered the room behind him. Frank put his hand on Charlie's arm, Elliott put her hand on the other. Ruby nosed her way through and angled her body right in front of Charlie.

"Where have you been, Frank?" Imogen asked. "I missed you."

Frank's voice was gentle. "I've been down here. You've got to listen to us. This place is not what it seems."

Not-Mom smiled. "He's right, Imogen. This place is so much more, so much better than the other one."

"Imogen, you could be stuck here," Charlie pleaded. "She's taking your memories. Your real ones, and replacing them with fake ones of her."

Imogen's eyes started to flicker between Not-Mom and Charlie, her brows drawn.

"I'm your real mom."

At those words, Charlie lunged, arms reaching.

But she was too fast for him. All he caught was air, and his palms hit square against the wall. The impact ricocheted through his body, "You aren't our real mom," Charlie spat.

He watched Imogen squeeze Not-Mom's hand a little tighter.

"Why is he doing this, Mom?" she asked. "Why doesn't he want us to all be together?" He hated the tremble in her voice. Hated that he'd caused it.

Before he turned around, he forced himself to take a deep breath in. He glanced at Elliott and Frank, who nodded in encouragement, and Ruby, who had her eyes trained on Not-Mom, her back legs bent like springs.

"He doesn't understand what I can give you both if you stay," Not-Mom said. "What this place can give to all of you." Her voice was warm and thick now, like his favorite blueberry syrup on pancakes. It coursed through his brain and slowed his thoughts. He didn't know why he had been so quick to jump at her.

Maybe he could listen for just a moment.

He turned. Not-Mom had already taken a step toward him. When Mom was worried about one of them, she'd have this crinkle in her left eye. Not-Mom had that same crinkle. Charlie had missed it—he hadn't been able to find it in any of his photographs.

"I know there are things that you don't want to remember," Not-Mom said. Her voice was soft. Understanding. "There are times you all don't want to remember."

Charlie looked back to Elliott and Frank again, though it felt like he was moving in slow motion. Their eyes were glassed over, too. Only Ruby's were still sharp and bright.

"What times?" Imogen said.

"Let's start with Charlie's. Remember how I looked at the end, tiny and frail, and you were afraid to come into the hospital room?" Charlie put his hands over his ears to block out the sound of her voice. Ruby began to howl.

Still, Not-Mom continued.

"And remember when I asked you to pick up Imogen from school because I was too sick and you forgot and she stayed there until you realized it when it was dark?" All his worst memories were on display.

Even though Ruby tried to block out Mom's voice for Charlie, it still wormed its way into his head. Probably because these memories were nothing new—he thought about them every day. They were part of him the same way his brain and lungs and veins and toes were part of him. Charlie wanted to apologize, wanted to go back in time and change things, and he couldn't. Waking up to that thought each morning made his stomach twist and turn.

He didn't realize it but now his hands were on his knees, and his body was shaking in this kind of violent way. He was slightly aware of a tugging on the back of his shirt. Then Not-Mom was right next to him, and there was Imogen in front of him. Her face was hopeful, her eyes wide. Not-Mom patted his hair like Mom used to. "There, there," she said. "I can make all those bad feelings go away, you know. We can replace the awful memories of things you did with good ones from down here, you and me and Imogen together. And Elliott and Jack. And Frank and Grandma."

Charlie's brain felt like it had been stuffed with cotton. The logical things that normally fit together like a puzzle scattered, and he couldn't piece anything together. All he knew was that his legs and arms and whole body were tired, as if he had been trudging about in wet clothes. And his heart ached in his chest, dull and throbbing.

Not-Mom was right. Things would be much easier here.

The tugging grew stronger. Charlie reached back and found a furry nose. Ruby let go and licked his palm. Once and then again. She shifted her body so that she wrapped around his knees, almost like a hug. With every move she made,

265

the cotton cleared a little and his view became sharper. He looked at Frank, at Elliott, at Ruby. At Imogen's outstretched hand as it came into focus. He grabbed it and held on.

He wasn't alone. That was what this other world wanted him to think. That he alone felt this kind of sadness. That only he felt crumpled inside. This world was the empty one. Charlie had been so focused on what had been that he had been blind to what was or what *could be.*

Memories of Mom were important. They were a part of him. Her love helped define who he was. But it also had to help him move forward. There were still memories to be made. With Frank and Elliott and the Mathletes. With Imogen. With Dad. With people who he didn't even know existed.

And Charlie's planet, which had tilted a little too far on its axis, righted itself. Things were clear now. It would be easier here, but it wouldn't be the same.

Charlie jerked back, just out of reach of Not-Mom. "No!" he said. "No! I am not Swiss cheese!" A strange battle cry, to be sure. But one that fit. One that was perfect. Charlie had to be a whole person, even if it hurt sometimes.

He had to think in inverse again. With Frank, the way to make him see, to fill in the bits that this world had subtracted out, was to remind him of their old memories together. Not-Mom's weapon seemed to be wielding memories they had together, both good and bad. The inverse of old was new.

And the new memories he and Imogen could create together were infinite.

He took Imogen by the shoulders, angling his body between hers and Not-Mom's. He crouched down to try to meet her gaze. "When we get home, we're going to go through an entire bag of Jelly Belly jelly beans and only eat the red ones and save the gross popcorn-flavored ones for Dad. Because he really likes them."

At Dad's name, Imogen met his eyes, and Ruby pressed her nose into her knee, pushing them closer together.

"And me and you and Frank are going to go out to the creek and build tiny boats for frogs just like you wanted. And we'll have a perfect day together—with tea cakes and vegetables cut up all fancy and violin music playing from the portable stereo." At this, Imogen's eyes grew brighter and wider like full moons. Not-Mom's face twisted. The ground beneath their feet began to shake.

Charlie danced out of the way of Not-Mom's lunging arms, barely dodging her, pulling Imogen along with him. But it seemed less like pulling now and more that he and Imogen's orbits were taking the exact same path again. "We'll make the cookies with the big chocolate chunks. Just like Mom used to do. And I know we might get eggshells in them, but that's okay because we'll be doing it together." Not-Mom's figure began to glow black and white as if she were made of television static.

Frank's and Elliott's eyes were once again focused. "We'll do science experiments in the front yard," Elliott cried. "And we'll find fossils in the creek and pretend we walked with the dinosaurs." Ruby's barks punctuated Elliott's words.

"And we'll do the hot wing challenge again," Frank said. "And this time I'll make it to double fire-engine hot."

The promise of new memories seemed to be taking away Not-Mom's power.

Her face and eyes flashed dark, overcome by shadows. Ruby snarled at Not-Mom's face. Her teeth bared as it flashed and morphed into Not-Grandma and Not-Jack and then back again.

Charlie let go of Imogen's shoulders and held his hand out this time. And even though her body shook and her lip trembled, she took it.

Not-Mom's shape began to disintegrate into a fine black dust. An increasing wind whipped it around his face, the tendrils trying to get into his nose, his eyes, his mouth. "Good memories. Bad memories. It doesn't matter," Charlie yelled, his voice almost swallowed up by the torrent.

Still, he held strong. He pulled Imogen into him, and she squeezed his hand.

"It doesn't matter because they're real!"

With those words, Not-Mom made one last desperate lunge at them, her fingertips circling Charlie's wrist, pulling him and Imogen apart and toward her into the swirling dust and ash. He tried to yank his arm away, but her grip tightened and he stumbled forward, farther away from everyone he loved. He twisted his wrist again, but Not-Mom held on. Her hold was too tight. Now Charlie could barely see Elliott and Frank and Imogen.

"Charlie!" Imogen yelled. She tried to grab onto the back of his shirt, but the fabric was ripped away.

"Charlie!" Frank and Elliott screamed, but his name was swallowed up in the wind.

But Ruby was ready. With one final ferocious growl, she took a running leap onto Not-Mom, knocking Charlie out of her grip. Ruby and Not-Mom tumbled to the ground, Ruby landing on top. Not-Mom tried to stand but Ruby spread out, shifting her weight, making sure she couldn't move.

"Ruby," Charlie cried. He reached out to her. "Ruby, no! Ruby, come!"

But Ruby stayed right where she was.

Charlie tried to take a step or two toward her, but the wind's direction had changed. Instead of pulling him closer, it pushed him away.

Ruby. It was because of Ruby. She was protecting them.

He fought against the wall of wind, calling her name. But

he couldn't get close enough. He couldn't get close enough.

Throughout everything, Ruby never took her eyes off him. And Charlie thought he saw her smile at him, as best a dog could anyhow.

THE BIRTH
OF STARS

A boom sounded, as if the earth itself had cracked in half, split right down the center, cutting straight through rock and magma and the iron core. It was the first of many. Each one was louder and more violent than the one before.

The second explosion blasted Charlie off his feet. He and Imogen flew about two yards and landed in a mess of legs and arms on the ground. He tried to position his body over hers to protect her from the blasts and covered her ears with his hands.

Sparks and heat flew out of Not-Mom's hands and toes. Each blast shot straight to the ceiling, rocketing out into the night sky through the opening in the dome. Her body of dust and shadow had turned into a fireworks display, Ruby absorbing each of the impacts. The light, the thunder. And it seemed that her white spots glowed even brighter until it looked like a constellation had formed on her very fur.

They had visited New York once, and one of Charlie's favorite things had been standing by the subway trains as they rushed by with a thunderous rumble. Every explosion felt like that, magnified. The bursts of light whizzed past him. His curls lifted—both from the wind and the electricity that buzzed in the air—and the back of his T-shirt blew upward, trying to make its escape.

Each flash left him blinded for a moment, but as his eyes adjusted, he looked across the room to try to gauge where everyone was.

The blasts came faster now. Huge fireballs in blue and red and green and yellow lit up the night. First came the whiz and then after a time, the boom as the fireball lodged itself into its rightful place in the sky. And with each boom came a stolen memory, returning to Charlie.

Boom. When he and Imogen made faces at the lion in his pen at the zoo and the lion roared back, making them jump about twenty feet.

Boom. The blanket forts they'd make in the family room to watch Mom's favorite movies from the nineties. They'd shut all the blinds to make the room super dark like a theater, and Mom would pop two giant bowls of popcorn and buy boxes of candy from Gas & Snacks for them to share.

Boom. Right after Mom was diagnosed, Charlie had gotten mad at her for something, and he had stomped around the house and said, "I hope you die" right to her face. He'd tried to take the words back, but they were already out there.

Boom. Mom's face glistening with tears (of laughter) as she looked up at Imogen and Charlie onstage in the St. Cecilia's Christmas pageant. Imogen played the part of a shepherd, and somehow Charlie had gotten the role of her sheep.

Boom. Boom. Boom. Charlie struggled against the force of the blasts to take one hand from Imogen's ear and wedge it over his heart. He wasn't sure how much more it could take—the rush of joy and sadness and love and anger. Years of memories—of his and Imogen's and Frank's and Elliott's—compacted into short bursts that rattled around in him and shook his insides with their force.

Charlie had read that the birth of stars was both violent and beautiful. He could never understand how those two things could be true at the very same time. The swirling of the cosmic dust, the intense pull of gravity, the heat, the eventual collapse.

But now he understood.

Life was like that, too. The great moments with Mom

could coexist with the ones he'd rather forget, but wouldn't. They'd push in on him and shape him, and after the force and the heat, he'd come out changed. Made of the same elements but different.

The blasts slowed—first separated by a few seconds and then a few more. Charlie timed it on his watch. One whole minute. Then two.

He looked up. Elliott was splayed out facedown on the other side. And Frank stood, his back to the wall, arms at his sides, as if he were riding one of those centrifugal force machines at the fair. His mouth was open wide and his eyes directed skyward.

Slowly, Charlie eased himself off Imogen. Her hair, full of static, stood up almost straight on end. He knelt down next to her. The echoes of the blasts still rang in his ears, and he couldn't quite figure out how loud he was talking, but he tried to whisper, "Are you okay?"

He held his breath.

Imogen picked her face off the ground. It was red and splotchy and there was a print on her skin in the shape of the floorboards. But she smiled, just a little, and nodded. He touched her shoulder and wasn't sure he could let go. She was real and she was there and Not-Mom—

Instinctively, he stretched his arms out to shield Imogen in case Not-Mom had somehow survived, ready to steal more of their real memories. But all that remained next to the golden telescope was a small pile of ash.

Charlie jumped up and pumped his fist in the air. "We did it!" he exclaimed.

He imagined this was better than winning States for Mathletes. Imogen was okay, and while his body was sore and achy, he still had all his limbs!

And Frank, who kind of resembled a fish with his open mouth, blinked once or twice. And Elliott and Ruby—

Elliott had crawled over to Ruby, her hand buried in her fur, her face hidden.

"Elliott?" he called. His voice still felt too loud. Too loud.

Elliott didn't turn around. She just shook her head once.

"Ruby?"

He waited. He waited for her tail to wag or her head to lift or her tags to jingle. But she didn't move. She didn't move and at once, Charlie was on the floor next to Elliott, and his hand was in Ruby's fur. Her soft white-and-black fur that looked like stars in the sky.

He worked his way to her heart. And left his hand there. Waiting. Waiting for the rise and fall. Waiting for a sign that she was okay.

It didn't come.

He felt Frank's hand on his back and Imogen's arm around his waist. "I'm sorry, Charlie," Frank said. His voice was hoarse. And after a moment Elliott's hand found his and she closed her fingers around his fingers. Charlie eased his head down so that his face was next to Ruby's.

"You saved me," he whispered. "You saved me."

His eyes prickled and burned, and soon there was a small rivulet of water running down his nose and into Ruby's fur. And Elliott's hand remained intertwined with his.

Life and death.

Beauty and violence.

MADE OF STARDUST

Charlie wanted to take Ruby with them. But it would have been impossible. She was too heavy, and it was too sad. So instead, they brought her outside and placed her in a space between the trees where she was in full view of the stars above, all of them back in their rightful places. Charlie knew she would have liked that.

They stopped at Frank's house first. Now that Not-Grandma was no longer a threat, he had something he needed to get: his gray cap. Charlie watched as Frank hugged it to his chest. But Frank didn't put it on—not yet.

Then they walked back to Elliott's house together, leaving the bikes behind. There was no need to rush now that the memories had been returned and the Echoes had been destroyed. Imogen had grabbed onto Charlie's hand tight. She was practically cutting off his circulation, but he didn't care. All he cared about was that they were together. Safe.

The hatch was waiting for them.

Charlie lifted Imogen in first, and then he helped Elliott in. They clung to either side with their arms. Frank wiped his palms on his pants and went in next. He let out a worried sigh.

"It'll work," Charlie reassured him. It had to work. They had come so far.

Charlie was the last in the hole. He swung there a minute, his legs free, and then said, "On the count of three, everyone. One, two, three."

All four of them lifted their arms, but they only bounced back up. Imogen whimpered.

"It's me," Frank said. His voice shook. "It's not letting us back because of me."

Frank tried to climb out of the hatch, but Charlie wouldn't let him. "We're all in this together," he said. He took a deep breath, though his arms were hot and tingly. Getting mad wouldn't solve anything. "Let's try again. One, two, three."

Again, the hatch rejected them. He had to think. This was a place of inverses, of opposites. Addition and subtraction.

Multiplication and division. To open up the hatch, Imogen had declared that she didn't want to live with Charlie and Dad, that she only wanted to be with Mom. Elliott had done the same thing with Jack.

Charlie had to say good-bye to what he couldn't have again and hello to the possibility of tomorrow. "I want to be with Dad," he started. "With Imogen and Frank and Elliott. With the Mathletes."

Imogen caught on. "And the play," she said. "I want to be Dorothy again."

"I want to be with all of you," Frank said. "With my mom and dad."

"I don't want to be anywhere but in the real world," Elliott said. "The four of us together."

Charlie braced himself again. This had to work. It had to. "Okay, one more time. On the count of three. One, two, three."

This time, when they let go, the hatch opened up and they zoomed through to the real world that awaited them on the other side.

Charlie was the last to emerge from the hole in the floor. Two hands wrapped around his and pulled him up the final bit, just when he felt like his noodle arms couldn't get him the rest of the way up. He landed in a heap on the floor and for a second, he let his cheek smoosh against the carpet.

He lifted his head and looked around the room. Imogen, splayed out on Elliott's beanbag chair. Frank and Elliott standing over him, grinning. Frank was still a bit paler than he used to be, and when he'd pulled Charlie up, his grip wasn't as strong. But there was the smallest spark of the old Frank in his eye and in the cap that had now taken its rightful place back on his head.

The clock on Elliott's dresser glowed 11:11. When he was younger, if he was up late enough, Mom would tell him to make a wish. And at this very moment, if he had been Before Charlie, he would have wished that Mom was still alive.

But this wasn't before, and he wasn't the same. So instead, because Mom always said that for wishes to come true they had to be heard, he said this: "I wish that everything would be okay."

Charlie knew that the word *okay* was a variable. When he was four, okay meant that he was supplied with a constant stream of watermelon Popsicles (the kind that pushed up out of their wrappers) and could go down the slide at Tiny Meadows as many times as he wanted. When he was nine, okay meant that he had the socks with the googly eyes and the felt spikes down the back for the Fifth Annual Crazy Sock Day at school and that he always got to eat his bag of chips before his sandwich at lunchtime.

And now, at twelve years and a month, okay meant that he and Imogen were together, that Dad would finally become a dad again, and that they would never forget Mom. Charlie knew that the memories of her might fade—even the brightest stars blinked out—but there were parts of Mom that were still a part of them.

The way Imogen liked to fold her pizza and how she bit on her pencil when she was thinking and the color of her hair and the way she loved words. And the way Charlie always seemed to trip over himself and the 100 percent probability that he would burn the cookies because he was too wrapped up in something else to check on them.

There had been this science special they had watched in class, and the narrator, in his booming narrator voice, said, "We are made of stardust," and then went on to explain how we are composed from the building blocks of stars—that the very elements that make us up, carbon and iron and oxygen, all were formed in the heart of a star.

Charlie and Imogen were made of stardust from Mom's burning constellation, which still pointed the way home.

OKAY

F rank, Imogen, and Charlie had left Elliott at her house with hugs and the smell of popcorn coming from the kitchen. Her mom was making it; it had been one of Jack's favorite things. Elliott thought maybe she and her mom could talk about it.

Now the three stood on Frank's front porch, staring at the door. The house was dark. Even the outside lights hadn't been turned on. But, even so, they could still see the tattered green Find Frank ribbon that his parents had tied on one of the posts.

"Question," Frank said. He turned to look at Charlie, shoving the hand that once hovered over the door, ready to knock, into the pocket of his jeans. "Am I ready?"

Charlie threw his arm around Frank's shoulder. "Short answer or long answer?"

"Long."

Charlie grinned. He could have guessed that. "Here's what I know. I know you're my best friend and when you were gone, I couldn't stand it. Sometimes I'd pick up the phone to call you and you wouldn't be there. And we couldn't be on Mathletes together or see the monster movie marathon together or any of that stuff. I'm ready to do all of that again with you." He paused. "And I think you are, too."

In response, Frank pulled Charlie into a hug.

"Remember," Imogen chimed in. "There's no place like home."

Mrs. Talley would have been proud. Imogen sounded like she really meant it.

Frank laughed. "Is this when I'm supposed to click my shoes together three times?"

Charlie shook his head. "You don't have to. You're already there."

Frank took a deep breath and pressed the doorbell. A chime sounded and a light flicked on. They could hear footsteps on the staircase and the click of the door as someone unlocked it.

Charlie squeezed Frank's shoulder a little tighter.

The door opened.

Charlie had never been more thankful to see the house. *His* house—stuffed full of mistakes and disappointments and unfolded laundry.

But also Mom—even though she wasn't there anymore, the house was still full of her. The red door, the flowers in the window box, the pictures, and the memories they'd made and the people she loved so much.

This house was real.

The front door was unlocked and the house was quiet except for a small sound coming from the family room.

Dad was sitting on the couch, his head in his hands, his shoulders shaking.

"Dad?" Imogen said. He looked up.

"Charlie, Imogen," he cried.

Imogen ran to him, throwing her arms around his neck. "We're here. We're home." She scooched next to him on the couch, leaving only a little space between them.

"I got your message," Dad said. "I came home as soon as I did. I drove around the neighborhood and I couldn't find you. I thought I'd lost you."

Charlie covered Imogen's legs with Mom's favorite blanket—the one he and Frank had *accidentally* unwound and then tried to knit back together with disastrous results. Imogen still had a smudge of ash on her ear, and the hair on the left side of her face had some weird kink to it from when she had lain on the ground.

Charlie went to shake the memory of that from his head but then stopped and nudged Imogen over just a bit with his shoulder. She folded up her knees, making room.

And they sat there—Charlie and Imogen and Dad—somehow fitting on a couch that had once seemed too small.

"Me and Imogen," Charlie said after a minute or two of quiet. "We're still here, Dad. We still need you."

Dad pushed his glasses back up his nose.

Charlie continued but concentrated on the TV straight ahead of him.

"A lot's happened to us. To our family." Charlie paused, wondering how much to say. "To me and Imogen. I wonder if it's been some kind of sign or message or something. From Mom or maybe even the universe. And Mom always said when the universe talks, you better listen."

"Your mother was a smart lady." Charlie could hear a smile in his voice.

And because it was one in the morning and he was tired, Charlie let it go at that, but he could feel the space between him and Dad and Imogen shrink even further. It could've been because the couch was old and saggy and two of the springs underneath the seat cushions were broken.

But Charlie was certain it was due to something else.

If Dr. Miller could have seen him now, he wondered what she'd write in her notebook.

Brave, maybe. *Okay kid. On his way.*

STELLA

*I*t had been three days since the hatch disappeared. Elliott's had disappeared, too. They still put heavy things over the space where they used to be, though, just in case.

Charlie rode past the bakery on the way to Elliott's in the afternoon after school. Her schedule wasn't quite as busy anymore, she told him. He stopped, leaning his bike against the light pole outside the bakery that had just pinged on. He cupped his eyes and leaned against the glass. Maybe Edna was still there. But now all he saw were empty display cases where cupcakes and homemade candies once sat. The door was covered with brown packing paper with a sign in the middle that said *Coming Soon*. Someone at his lunch table said it was going to be a taco place. He'd have to tell Frank about it. Dr. Miller said he was coming back for a half day next Tuesday. He was going to start out slow before coming back to school full-time. But he was going to the Mathletes' lunch practice. With Charlie.

Charlie liked tacos. They reminded him of the Mexican fiesta nights they used to have and how Mom would play mariachi music from the record player as they danced around the kitchen. It was a memory worth holding on to.

He just wished he could've had the memory of saying a proper good-bye to Edna, too.

That night, Charlie, Dad, and Imogen sat at the kitchen table. Charlie smiled as Imogen waved her fork in the air, bits of corn flying out of her mouth as she recounted some dramatic story from play practice that day. She wasn't Dorothy anymore, but Mrs. Talley had fit her in again, and Imogen was thrilled. Dad didn't say much, but he did compliment the potatoes—the kind that Charlie had made from the box. One day, Charlie would learn how to make Mom's, but for today, this was enough.

Later, just as Imogen had passed him the last dish to rinse off in the sink, there was a knock at the door. Charlie glanced at the clock—8:05. Imogen threw the towel onto the counter and sprinted to the door. "I'll get it," she yelled.

Charlie set the dish on the drying rack and followed her down the hall.

Imogen stood in the front entry, door wide open to the yard and the street beyond that and the night sky just beyond that. But he didn't see anyone.

"Is someone there?" Charlie asked. He followed with: "Did we get a package?" even though it was too late for deliveries.

"Kind of," she said. She pointed toward the front step. "Look!"

On the porch was a brown woven basket lined with a blanket. And on that blanket sat a tiny black dog with a ruby-red collar. It looked up at them with its big eyes in a way that almost seemed familiar, reflecting the stars above.

"It looks like she's been dusted with powdered sugar," Imogen exclaimed. She knelt down and gently gathered the puppy in her arms. Charlie touched it, right under its chin. The dog closed its eyes and seemed to melt into him, just as Ruby had. "Dad! Dad! There's a dog at our door, and I really think we're meant to keep it. People don't leave puppies on your porch randomly, you know!" This, Charlie knew, was true.

Imogen and Charlie charged into the family room, nearly tripping over a startled Dad, who clicked off the TV. Imogen almost shoved the puppy in his face. Dad and the puppy stared at each other, sizing each other up. Then, in the very next moment, it licked him right across the nose with its impossibly long tongue.

A sound came from Dad's mouth that Charlie almost didn't recognize. It took him a second and then it registered—Dad had just laughed.

Imogen turned a silver disc hanging from the collar over in her hands. "Her name is Stella," she said.

Stella. Star. Charlie rushed back to the door and onto the front porch.

"Edna!" he called.

And at the far end of the street, just before the road disappeared over the hill, Charlie could have sworn he saw an old woman hunched over a bicycle. And if he squinted just right and turned his head twenty-seven degrees to the left, he thought he could see her gray hair polka-dotted with white.

As she disappeared into the horizon, Charlie looked up into the sky. There was a cluster of stars he hadn't noticed before. He'd have to check his star map later, but he was sure of it.

He thought back to that one conversation with Elliott in her room about naming the constellations. Charlie had found his.

Ruby the brave. Imprinted in the sky.

Hers was a story worth telling.

ACKNOWLEDGMENTS

This book wouldn't be a book without the support, enthusiasm, and hard work of a whole team of people. I would like to offer my thanks and gratitude to:

My agent, Victoria Marini, who is made of magic—the good kind. For your support, guidance, and belief in me and in Charlie Price, I am so grateful.

My editor, Alessandra Balzer, who is as brilliant as she is kind. She saw the heart of this book and helped me reveal it. Every writer needs an Alessandra in her corner. I am so thankful she is in mine.

The amazing Kelsey Murphy, Viana Siniscalchi, Nellie Kurtzman, Jenna Lisanti, Megan Barlog, Caroline Sun,

Ruiko Tokunaga, Josh Weiss, Mark Rifkin, Alexei Esikoff, Valerie Shea, Andrea Pappenheimer, Kerry Moynagh, Kathy Faber, Katie Fitch, Amy Ryan, Barb Fitzsimmons, and the rest of the team at Balzer + Bray and HarperCollins. Charlie and I are so lucky to have such enthusiastic, knowledgeable, and passionate people on our side.

Melissa Baumgart, my writing friend turned real-life friend, for your support, incredible insight, and ceaseless enthusiasm; Dee Romito, my very first writing friend—I am so thrilled we are celebrating our debut year together; and to Janet Sumner Johnson, for your keen eye and encouragement on this book.

My writing group—Ailynn Knox-Collins, Anne Cunningham, Tina Hoggatt, Heather Lehr, and Lily LaMotte. Pom-poms!

The Sweet Sixteens debut group—your support has been invaluable. Special thanks to Ruth Lehrer for our many, many emails! I am glad I can count you not only as a fellow writer but a friend.

Writing teacher extraordinaires Micol Ostow, Corey Ann Haydu, and Kurtis Scaletta. Thank you for being so giving of your encouragement, time, and writing knowledge. You taught me how to tell a better story. There are not enough words to thank you, but hopefully these are a start.

Craig Niemi at the Cincinnati Observatory. Thank you

for answering my questions about the layout of the observatory and the telescopes housed there. While I have taken some liberties in the telling of this story, I hope that everyone will visit this Cincinnati gem.

Hank and Oliver—my four-legged writing buddies. Your unconditional love served as the inspiration for Ruby's.

My former students at St. Brigid of Kildare School in Ohio. You are inspiring and smart and kind. I love writing books for kids like you.

My extended family. Special thanks to my mom: I had a childhood that was never short on books or love.

My husband, Kurt—for your love and your belief in me. I am so grateful for all of the memories we already share and I'm looking forward to the ones we still get to create together. You are the very best.

Finally, my dad and sister—this book is in memory of both of you. I just wish you could be here to read it.